THE DEVIL'S BABY
JOHNITA M. SMITH

THE DEVIL'S BABY

JOHNITA M. SMITH

THE DEVIL 'S BABY

Copyright @ 2025 Johnita M. Smith
ISBN: 979-8-9919922-6-8
All rights reserved.

Library of Congress Cataloging-in-Publication Data

Editing: SynergyEd Consulting/ synergyedconsulting.com
Graphics & Cover Design: Greenlight Creations Graphics Designs
glightcreations.com/ glightcreations@gmail.com

shero.
Publishing
SHEROPUBLISHING.COM

DEDICATION

To my mother...

THE DEVIL'S BABY

PART ONE

CHAPTER ONE

ALONE

CHAPTER ONE
Alone

Momma always said, "Baby, it's just us. You and me. We don't have any other family. Sadly, they're gone to heaven." But when I asked why—what happened—she would only say, "Ebony, it was God's will."

I never understood. How could we not have any other family on the planet? Why would God do such a thing? But that was the truth—or at least, that's what Momma told me. She always said not to question God because that's how you make Him mad. Even as a child, I knew that wasn't a good thing.

In grade school, I secretly hoped God would answer my prayers, that He would heal the emptiness I was born with. But He never did. No one ever showed up for my little performances or to celebrate the holidays with us. It was always just me and Momma. Sometimes she'd notice how lonely I looked, and to make me feel special, she would say:

"Baby girl, you are different. We are not like everyone else. You have to protect your energy."

Protecting my energy was something I eventually got really good at. I trusted Momma. I clung to every word that left her mouth. She loved me, and that was enough. So, I stopped asking questions. I stopped bothering God with my prayers—He clearly had more important things to do. Even if I secretly wished for more family, they never came, so Momma had to be right.

She always seemed to know what I was thinking. "I hear you over there," she'd say. "I know what you're thinking. But one day, you're gonna look back and be thankful that it's just us. Not all family is good family. Don't ever forget that. Even when we don't understand why things are the way they are, God knows best."

I accepted her explanations. I adapted to her logic because she was my everything. It was me and Momma for life. I loved everything about her—her smile, her infectious laugh—and please don't get me started on her cooking! Even though we didn't have much, she always made sure I had enough.

Momma—Elaine Blake—was a beauty. At forty, she had caramel skin and a head full of dark, reddish-brown curls, always pinned up in her favorite chic updo. She took pride in herself, in how she looked, and she never ate food from other people's houses. She exercised, meditated, and read constantly. She was also cautious. Overly cautious. She didn't like to be around too many people, and she raised me the same way.

"Ebony, mind your business and keep your distance."

"Ebony, don't get too close to people. The same ones that smile in your face will stab you in your back."

"Honey, know that you are valuable. If those kids don't want to be your friend, that's their loss. They did you a favor."

I never told her, but sometimes, late at night, I would wake up and hear her crying softly. She had no idea I was watching. Even though she enjoyed her peace, I knew she missed the family she said God had taken from her. But whenever I asked her about it the next day, she would brush it off—pretend like I was mistaken. And then, just like that, she was gone.

The next morning was still. The day felt alien. I woke up in a foreign land. The weight of reality sat on my chest like cement. Grief tasted like hot lead on my tongue. "I don't know if I can do this," I thought. "How am I supposed to do this without you, Ma?"

Tears had dried on my face, my eyes swollen tight from crying all night. I was afraid to touch them, afraid they might bleed from the grief. Bleed from the sadness. Bleed from the overwhelming loss. All I could remember was Principal Lee standing before a sea of blue caps, announcing, "Let's rise to celebrate the Class of 2000, the 'new millennials!' You did it, kids! Congratulations!" Hats filled the air. Laughter, cheers. I hugged Charlotte, my best friend, as her parents showered her with gifts.

And then I looked for Momma.

She was always there for me. Always. I waited, scanning the crowd for her familiar smile. I needed to see her arms stretched wide, ready to embrace me like she always did when I accomplished something big. But then came the sirens.

The McDillion police walked straight toward me. The crowd split in two. My heartbeat thundered in my ears as the female deputy said my name. And then she told me. Everything blurred. My body moved on autopilot as I followed them to the hospital to identify my mother's body.

How could things change so fast? Just days ago, all I could think about was graduating top of my class and making Momma proud. I had dreams—big dreams—of becoming a nurse, of following in her footsteps. But all of that was gone now. I had never known pain like this. I had to get up and get dressed for Momma's memorial service today. I promised myself I wouldn't give up, but I wasn't sure if that was a promise I could keep.

Home Alone

The doorbell rang.

At first, I just laid there, pretending I didn't hear it. But the ringing didn't stop. Whoever was at the door wasn't giving up. I rolled off the bed, reached for my Hello Kitty robe, and shuffled toward the door. The neon glow of my alarm clock read **7:00 AM**. Don't they know I'm in here? Where else would I be?

RING. RING.

"I'm coming!" I called, my voice hoarse.

I peered through the stained-glass window of the front door and saw a much-needed face: Charlotte Goodman. My best friend. I should have called her back days ago, but I couldn't bring myself to do it. I took a deep breath before opening the door.

"Charlotte, I'm so—"

"Don't you even think about apologizing, Ebony Blake." She stepped inside, throwing her arms around me. "I can barely sleep or eat. I can't imagine what you're going through. My parents made me give you space, but I had to see you."

Tear stains bruised her cheeks, mirroring my own. We slid to the floor in the foyer, holding each other like the world was caving in.

"Ebony, it's all over the local news. Nothing like this has ever happened in our town. My parents are worried about you, especially my mom. How are you holding up here alone? Do you need anything?"

"Char... I don't know what to do. I've never lived without her. I've never breathed without her. What am I supposed to do?"

Charlotte didn't have an answer. But she held me, and in that moment, that was enough.

The Morgue

Elaine Blake's body lay still on the cold examination table. The forensic pathologist took his time, noting the bruises on her arms, legs, and knuckles.

"She was a fighter," he murmured. "Whoever did this, they didn't leave unscathed." Detective Carter stepped closer. "Did she have any DNA under her nails? Any evidence?"

"No. The killer wore gloves. But there's something else..." The examiner hesitated, then turned Elaine's head slightly, exposing the back of her neck. Burned into her skin was a crescent moon. And across both her wrists, deep carved crosses.

Detective Carter exhaled sharply. "This wasn't random. This was a message."

For the first time in forty years, the examiner felt a chill run down his spine. Something dark had come to McDillion, Georgia. And it wasn't finished yet.

CHAPTER TWO

MEMORIAL

CHAPTER TWO
Memorial

The memorial service, led by Pastor Johnson from my mother's church, McDillion Baptist, was small and private—just as I had requested. Pastor Johnson knew my mother well. He was an older man, likely in his seventies, standing six feet tall with dark brown skin and a neatly shaved salt-and-pepper beard and mustache. He was dressed impeccably in a black suit and matching tie. But when the wind blew, the sweet, familiar scent of his cologne carried to me, bringing tears to my eyes. It had been my mother's favorite fragrance. I remembered how she would linger after church just to greet him, savoring the scent on her cheek as she walked home.

"Young Ebony Blake, the Lord has not left you alone. He still has a plan for your life, daughter. I am always here for you, for counsel and prayer, just as I was for Elaine," he said, walking up to me and taking my hand at the end of the service.

"Is it okay if I come by and visit? Just to check on you, of course."

"Thank you, Pastor Johnson. I'd like that in the coming weeks, if you don't mind," I responded softly.

"Honey, I don't mind at all. Take your time and stay close to God. He will never give you more than you can handle. I know it doesn't feel like it now, but God will bring you through this. Don't lose faith."

With his strong, sweet-smelling arms, Pastor Johnson embraced me tightly. In that moment, all I could think of was my mother—how much she would have cherished this warmth.

Away from the crowd of my mother's friends, church members, and coworkers stood a man I didn't recognize. He was tall—around six-foot-one—and dressed in a dark gray three-piece suit. In his hand, he clutched a bouquet of yellow roses—my mother's favorite. A black brimmed hat was tilted just enough to shadow his face from a distance. He faced the memorial but chose not to join.

I wondered who he was and how he knew my mother. His skin was lighter than hers, and as I watched him wipe his eyes, I could tell by his body language that he was deeply affected. He had known her. He had cared for her.

"Who's that guy?" Charlotte whispered beside me.

"I have no idea. I was just wondering the same thing. But it looks like he knew Mama."

"Why do you say that?" she asked.

"Because he brought her favorite flowers. Yellow roses made her smile, but my mother was a private person. He had to have known her well to know that."

Charlotte smirked. "Well, well. Looks like your mother had some secrets. Including a 'boo.' He's kinda old, but hey— maybe that was her type."

"Yep. And he looks like he got money. You know Mama—she definitely knew her worth," I replied.

After the service, the church mothers from McDillion Baptist held a dinner for Mama at our house. Mrs. Goodman helped in the kitchen while Charlotte and I sat outside on the back porch, inhaling the fresh air. Not far from us, the half-opened kitchen window let voices drift through the blinds.

The kitchen, though small, had character. Original hardwood floors squeaked in certain places, and black-and-white tile countertops gave it charm. Mama had decorated it with a cow motif to match the counters, but the only photos on the fridge were of the two of us.

"Well, I guess we're done in here, Sister Johnson. The pastor held a beautiful memorial service for Miss Elaine. I still can't believe she's gone."

"I know what you mean, Sister Bradley. The older I get, the more I realize that life isn't promised to anyone, no matter how old or young," the pastor's wife said sadly. "But my heart aches for that child. She doesn't deserve to be left alone like this."

"Dear God, losing your mother is horrific at any age, but at seventeen…" Sister Bradley choked on her words. "I don't know what I'd do."

"Sister Goodman, thank you so much for stepping up and helping young Ebony through this overwhelming grief. God sees your kindness," the pastor's wife added.

"Thank you. I'm only doing what I'd hope someone would do for my baby if the shoe were on the other foot. Ebony has always been sweet, and her friendship with my Charlotte has been like medicine since we lost baby William ten years ago."

Sister Johnson nodded. "Yes indeed, I remember those dark days. But look at you now—Mayor of McDillion and a champion for women in this town. We're proud of you, Gladys."

"But Mayor Goodman," Mrs. Erica Bradley's voice lowered, moving closer to the covered window. "What really happened to Elaine? Is it true she was killed in a hit-and-run?"

"Hit-and-run? No." The pastor's wife sighed. "I heard from others in the church that it looked like something… out of this world."

"Out of this world? You mean, like the devil?" Sister Bradley whispered.

Mayor Goodman hesitated. "Ladies, I can't share too much."

"Not even with your largest donors?" the pastor's wife countered.

"And your most loyal supporters?" Mrs. Bradley added.

Mayor Goodman exhaled. "From what the police chief showed me, it was an unusual attack on someone we all knew in our community. That's all I'll say—for Ebony's sake."

"Unusual? Why would he say that?" Sister Johnson pressed.

"There were no witnesses in the parking lot at the time Elaine left the hospital. But as soon as she got to her car, she was attacked—and later found in the woods not far from the location."

The two women gasped, glancing at each other in alarm.

"Poor Ebony," Sister Johnson murmured. "Her mother was kind, but an outsider. Pastor and I met her when she moved into the Wickum's old house, but she barely came to church. We didn't know her well."

"Did the chief say if she had next of kin?" Mrs. Bradley asked.

"They're looking into it. I plan to help." Mayor Goodman paused. "Did you know Elaine was from Virginia?"

"Virginia?" Both women looked surprised.

"Yes." Mayor Goodman nodded. "But don't worry—I'll make sure Ebony is taken care of."

Sister Johnson placed a hand on her shoulder. "May the good Lord bless you for looking after that child. You're exactly what this town needs, Mayor Goodman. I'll make sure the pastor knows."

"Thank you. I need all the blessings I can get in this new role," the mayor said, unaware of the listening ears on the back porch.

My wide eyes locked with Charlotte's as we absorbed the conversation.

"Charlotte… did your mama just say my mother had family?" I whispered, my voice shaking.

Charlotte inhaled deeply. "Ebony, take a deep breath with me, bestie. No—what my mama said was your mother was from Virginia, not Georgia."

"And here I thought this mayor position had gotten to her head a little. How's she gonna spill my bestie's tea and not tell me first?" Charlotte scoffed.

"There must be some mistake," I muttered. "Mama told me years ago that her family died in a storm when she was a young girl. That's why she moved here, put herself through nursing school, and built our life."

Charlotte shot me a skeptical look. "If they died in a storm, there should be records of it."

My head swam. "First, my mama had a boyfriend I didn't know about. Now, she's from Virginia? This day just keeps getting worse."

Charlotte's expression shifted. She had that look—like she was onto something. And I knew my best friend well enough to know she wasn't letting this go.

OLD FRIENDS

CHAPTER THREE
Old Friends

Laketown, Virginia, was a town built over 150 years ago along Freedmen Lake. A bridge crossed the lake, leading to Old Laketown, a historic Victorian-style Black community. The neighborhood, nearly two centuries old, held deep roots and stories of resilience.

In a small home in Old Laketown, an elderly mother and her adult daughter enjoyed a simple breakfast in their living room, eating from handcrafted wooden dinner trays while watching the morning news. Mary Woods, known in the community for her natural herbs and fresh vegetables, sold her produce at local markets. A practice passed down through generations of Woods Women—Black women gifted by blood with knowledge of the earth's healing powers.

The Woods Women traced their lineage back to enslaved women on the Lakely plantation. When they were raped and tortured by their masters, they delivered their cursed babies deep in the pine woods, their blood seeping into the soil, turning it into blood clay. Their suffering forged a spiritual connection with the earth, a bond that strengthened over time. To this day, the Woods Women possessed an innate ability to grow and identify plants with powerful healing properties.

Mary's only daughter, Cheryl, took after her father rather than following the Woods Women's traditions. Cheryl was an ex-sergeant in the local police force, now working as a private investigator. She had left the force with one goal in mind—to solve the case of her father's murder, a case that had gone cold for over twenty years.

"So, do you have any plans today, daughter? Tell me how business has been lately," Mary asked, her voice warm and knowing.

"Everything is going okay, Ma. I'll check my emails, see if anyone's reached out lately." Cheryl's eyes flickered to the television. "Ma, can you turn that up? Looks like something went down in Georgia."

The old woman reached for the remote and turned up the volume. The news anchor spoke about an unresolved murder.

"In McDillion, Georgia, police are seeking assistance in solving the murder of Elaine Blake, a nurse at McDillion Hospital. Blake was attacked and killed after her evening shift; her body found hours later deep in the woods. Authorities report she was abducted near her car by an unknown assailant before being murdered. Her colleagues describe her as a hardworking, dedicated nurse with no known enemies. The mayor of McDillion issued a statement earlier today."

A clip played of Mayor Gloria Goodman addressing the town. "We are all deeply shocked by this tragedy. I knew Elaine personally, and my office will be working closely with the McDillion Police Department to ensure her family receives justice. Please keep her daughter in your prayers."

"If you have any information, please call the number at the bottom of the screen."

"That's so sad," Mary murmured, shaking her head. "So many monsters in the world, honey. You've got to be careful when you're dealing with other people's problems."

Cheryl's expression darkened. "Ma, didn't that woman look familiar?"

Mary frowned. "You know, now that you mention it, she reminds me of Violet. Her eyes, her facial structure..."

"Yeah. She looks like Miss Bridges."

Cheryl stood abruptly, her mind racing.

"Ma, do you know what I'm thinking right now?"

"Oh Lord," Mary sighed. "I can only imagine."

"Ma... what if that woman was Evelyn?"

Mary's face twisted in disbelief. "Evelyn Bridges? Cheryl, she died twenty years ago."

"But they never found her body."

Mary pursed her lips. "Cheryl, I remember they had to have a closed-casket funeral. They said her injuries were too horrific."

"No, Ma. I remember rumors that there was no body inside that casket. That it was all for show."

Mary's face darkened. "Cheryl, I don't need you stirring up old wounds with the Bridges family. Miss Violet has been a long-time customer. She practically kept me in business during that harsh winter season."

"I know, Ma, but Evelyn was my friend. I was so upset when she disappeared. I always knew something was off. I just couldn't do anything about it."

Mary exhaled deeply. "Yes, I remember, Cheryl. Because not long after that, your father was killed. That was a dark time in Old Laketown."

Cheryl nodded. "That's why I became a cop. I wanted to make a real difference."

Mary reached out, placing a gentle hand on her daughter's arm. "You know, I used to worry about you. You have the Woods Women's gift, but you chose another path. Your father always told me not to worry—that you'd find your own way."

Cheryl smiled wistfully. Her father had always believed in her, no matter what.

"I know you miss him," Mary continued. "But you can't live your life for him. You have to find your own way to your purpose."

Cheryl had heard those words a thousand times. "It's in your blood."

"Just promise me one thing," Mary pleaded. "Don't let this path lead you to an early grave."

Cheryl met her mother's gaze and nodded. But as she scribbled down the tip-line number from the television screen, she knew—she had just found her next case.

"Thank you for calling the McDillion Police Department. How can I help you?"

"Yes, could you transfer me to Officer Rebecca Landon's desk?"

"May I ask who's calling?"

"Sgt. Woods."

"Please hold."

Cheryl's heart pounded. It had been years since she had spoken to Rebecca. Their breakup had been mutual, but she still missed their conversations—their friendship. She had been surprised when she found out Rebecca had transferred to McDillion PD. She had never told her mother about their relationship, but she always felt Mary knew.

A familiar voice came on the line. "Now, there's only one Sergeant Woods I know, and she's no longer in the force. Cheryl, how are you?"

Cheryl exhaled, smiling. "Rebecca. It's so good to hear your voice."

Rebecca chuckled. "What's up? This is out of the blue."

"I need to talk to you about a case."

"Which one?"

"Elaine Blake." Rebecca sighed. "Ah, the spooky case."

"Spooky? Why do you say that?"

"It's the strangest case I've ever worked."

"Well, I think I have some information. I want to talk to the right person about it. Can you get me in touch with Mayor Goodman?"

Rebecca hesitated, then replied, "Yeah. She's solid. I just sent you her number."

Cheryl felt a surge of excitement. "Thanks, Rebecca. And hey—don't be a stranger."

Rebecca's voice softened. "I won't. Stay safe, Cheryl."

The Goodmans

At River Ridge, an upscale gated community in McDillion, Mayor Gloria Goodman sat in her home office, reflecting on the day. The brutality of Elaine's murder haunted her. Every time she closed her eyes, she saw the bruises, the slashed wrists, the branding on her neck. It felt like something out of a horror movie. Her phone rang, pulling her from her thoughts.

"Hello, Goodman residence."

"Yes, hello, may I speak with Mayor Gloria Goodman?"

"Speaking. May I ask who's calling?"

"My name is Cheryl Woods. I'm a private investigator from Laketown, Virginia."

"Okay… and how can I help you, Miss Woods?"

"I think I can help you."

Mayor Goodman's brow furrowed. "Go on."

"I have information that will turn this case upside down."

CHAPTER FOUR

THE REVEAL

CHAPTER FOUR
The Reveal

"Mayor Goodman, let me tell you a story about a dark time in Laketown…"

"Wait, Laketown, Virginia?" the mayor asked abruptly.

"Yes," Cheryl responded. "But have you ever heard of the mysterious elite neighborhood that extends from Laketown? It's called Old Laketown."

"You know, I have. There was an all-Black university there that was a big deal back in the day."

"Absolutely," Cheryl agreed. "But it was absorbed into the prestigious Laketown University in the fifties after schools were integrated. Old Laketown University was actually the first HBCU built and established by Black Americans. The leaders of Old Laketown University sold the land to big investors from the state of Virginia, which led to the building of Laketown University. However, the Black elites were able to negotiate the rights to their school, maintaining total control over their teaching and curriculum. On campus, they have their own buildings and sorority. The leaders of the institution are the foundational Black families, direct descendants of the Lakely plantation. These families were the real leaders, establishing their wealth during the Freedmen's era. They built their fortune into the millions."

"Really?" The mayor nodded thoughtfully. "I didn't know that. I remember my parents and grandparents talking about that all-Black university in Virginia when I was a young girl. It was a big deal and kind of a secret as well," she implied. "But please continue. I apologize for interrupting."

"Well, about twenty years ago, the five Black founding families were attacked, and each family lost a daughter."

"Wait a minute—each family lost a child? How?" The mayor caught herself mid-sentence. "Oh, shoot, I interrupted again, didn't I? I'm sorry. I'll try harder. Please go on."

"Right," Cheryl said with slight hesitation. "That year, each family had a daughter who pledged in Old Laketown College's oldest and most elite sorority, The Divine Daughters. The class of eighty-one was special because their initiation ceremony fell on the blood moon, and there was a prophecy that the church and the families believed would be revealed. One of the daughters would gain the power of God and the devil through the transferable power of the moon."

"Okay, Miss Woods, this is an interesting story, but what does all of this have to do with this case?"

"I'm happy you asked. Like I said, twenty years ago, five of the twelve young ladies who pledged that year died in a freak accident on campus. There was a huge funeral and mourning for the small town of Old Laketown. But only one girl had a closed casket. Her name was Evelyn Bridges. She was said to have been the daughter of dark power, the one who was supposed to be the anointed one. But you know her as Elaine Blake."

"Wait, what…"

The Goodman Women

With sudden shock and disbelief, Charlotte's reaction to what she had just heard caused her to slightly punch the door. Her observant mother, quick and quiet, grabbed the handle before it could make too much noise. While Cheryl was still talking on the other end of the line, Charlotte had been discovered eavesdropping on her mother's conversation, learning information that was neither her business nor what her mother felt was her concern.

Mayor Goodman quickly ended the conversation with PI Woods by inviting her to McDillion for a couple of days. They decided to revisit the information later. The mayor promised to call back to schedule their meeting but welcomed Private Investigator Woods on board to assist with solving the case.

"What exactly are you doing, Charlotte? Why are you sneaking around my office, listening in on my private conversations? You do know that I have a very important job in this city, right?"

"Yes, ma'am. I was going to knock, but the phone rang, and I didn't want to bother you. But when I heard that lady's voice, it reminded me of Miss Elaine. I'm sorry for snooping, but is what she said true? Was Ebony's mother some kind of witch or something?"

"No, Elaine Blake was not a witch," the mayor responded firmly.

"Then why are people saying weird things about her death?" Charlotte asked curiously.

"Honey, don't listen to the gossip of others. Especially people who don't have a clue what they're talking about."

Charlotte approached her mother's desk and leaned in with sincerity and concern. "Mom, when I leave for Spelman next week, promise me that you will watch out for Ebony. She is all alone, and I just can't imagine what she's going through on so many levels. Just thinking about how much her life has changed this past week… I haven't even spoken to her about me leaving for college because, in a way, I feel bad. My life has always been so good in comparison to hers, and it makes me feel awful inside. I know it's not my fault how things have turned out, but I just want us to help her in any way we can. Please."

Tears slowly fell from Charlotte's eyes as she spoke in confidence. She very seldom showed this compassionate side of herself, but her mother understood and responded with the same tenderness her daughter had shown.

"Honey, as you become an adult, you will learn that life can bring unexpected circumstances. Sometimes, things happen that completely change the plans you thought you had for yourself. But the last thing your father and I want is for you to carry other people's burdens on your shoulders. I promise you, I will help Ebony get a fresh start, and we will always be there for her, to support her and uplift her."

"Thank you, Mom. I know you will make it happen," Charlotte said with a smile.

"Well, you know, when the Goodman women put their minds to something, we win every time," the mayor responded.

"Absolutely. And we don't play about that," Charlotte said, wiping her eyes and taking a deep breath of relief.

"Now, go and be excited about your future. You have worked extremely hard to get into Spelman. Since you were a little girl, it has been your dream to graduate from Spelman," Mayor Goodman reminded her.

"Remember, daughter, you are a Goodman woman. We win every time."

"Yes, ma'am, every time!" Charlotte affirmed with conviction.

Miss Dee's Diner

Miss Dee's Diner had been a staple across the tracks since the early sixties. Mayor Goodman, sitting in a comfy coffee-colored pleather booth that seated four, waited patiently for her guest to arrive while sipping a fresh cup of coffee. The diner was a big part of her childhood. With every warm sip of joe, she reminisced about meeting her girlfriends here in high school and how they would gather after school to enjoy Miss Dee's famous milkshakes. She chuckled, thinking about how she and Robert had their first date right here in the corner booth.

Mayor Goodman loved this place, and when she found out that people were trying to put Miss Dee out of business, she knew she had to do something to make a change in her community.

"Honey, do you need anything?" Miss Dee asked, interrupting the mayor's thoughts.

"Oh no, Miss Dee. I'm waiting on someone, but she might be hungry when she arrives. If you could check back with us then, I'd appreciate it," the mayor said respectfully.

"Of course, Mayor Goodman. You know you will always be taken good care of here. You've always been like a daughter to me. I really appreciate everything you've done for this place. I haven't had the chance to thank you since you took office."

"You're so welcome, Miss Dee. As long as I'm here, this place will always be in good hands. You just keep doing what you do—making this community better every day these lights are on. We need you, Miss Dee."

"Thank you so much, Gloria. I really appreciate you. It hasn't always been easy since my husband passed, but my oldest son and two daughters are helping me run the place now. It's officially a family business. Because of you and your administration going out of your way to help Black-owned businesses in McDillion, we are here to stay," Miss Dee said, tears forming in her elderly eyes.

"God bless you and your family, Miss Dee," the mayor said warmly.

"I'll see you in church on Sunday, yes, ma'am?" Miss Dee asked.

"Yes, ma'am," the mayor replied.

"Good, honey," Miss Dee said as she slowly walked back to her corner office. Her adult daughters continued tending to customers and keeping the historic diner clean.

The front door opened, and a slender-built, brown-skinned woman with black micro locs styled in a neat bob walked in. She was professionally dressed in a white button-down blouse, black trousers, and a black blazer. She moved with confidence in her black flats, a medium-sized black leather tote bag strapped across her chest. Scanning the room, she locked eyes with the mayor and approached her with a smile.

"Good morning, Mayor Goodman," she said, extending her hand.

The mayor slowly rose, shaking her hand in a professional manner.

"Yes, good morning, Miss Woods. I'm so happy you made it safely. Welcome to McDillion, Georgia."

"Thank you so much for having me. I was very happy to hear back from you so soon, and I'm ready to get to work on this case. This diner was very easy to find."

"Yes, well, for someone who's never been to my small town, I thought I'd start you off at our historic Black diner—Miss Dee's Diner—the best food and milkshakes in town," the mayor said proudly.

As P.I. Woods took a few seconds to admire the beautiful Black art on the walls and inhale the mouthwatering aroma in the air, Delilah, Miss Dee's oldest daughter, approached the booth to take their order. She wore a black Miss Dee's Diner t-shirt with a bright-colored name tag.

"Good morning, ladies. Can I get you something to drink?"

"Yes, thank you, Delilah. I'll have a refill. What would you like, Miss Woods?" the mayor asked.

"Yes, I'll have hot tea with honey, please."

"We have green, breakfast blend, and Earl Grey. Which would you like?" Delilah asked.

"I'll take the breakfast blend and a breakfast sandwich with bacon, thank you," P.I. Woods said, glancing at the menu.

"Okay, I'll be back with your hot tea and honey. Your breakfast sandwich will be out as soon as possible," Delilah said, retrieving the menus from the table.

As soon as Delilah was out of sight, the mayor leaned in, lowering her voice.

"I can't stop thinking about our conversation yesterday. It doesn't make sense, but you have a very interesting perspective on the victim. I'm eager to hear how you put this together, Miss Woods."

"Mayor Goodman, I know this seems crazy, but I'm telling you the truth—and I came with proof today," Cheryl said, reaching for her black leather tote bag. Inside were vanilla-colored files filled with papers, photographs, and newspaper articles. She flipped through them and pulled out a folder labeled *Evelyn Bridges.*

Before she could open it, Delilah returned.

"Here you are, ma'am—hot breakfast tea and honey," she said.

"Thank you so much, Delilah," the mayor replied.

Cheryl moved the tea and honey to the side and, once Delilah was gone, opened the file and turned it towards the mayor.

"Here is all the proof you need. Take a second and let me know what you think."

The mayor placed her coffee mug down gently and took her time reading through the file on *Evelyn Bridges.* Her eyes widened in shock as she looked at a familiar yet youthful face— the mother of her daughter's best friend, Elaine Blake, aka *Evelyn Bridges.*

The file contained four pages. The first showed a younger photo of Evelyn and details about her family and background. The second page covered the other victims and the police's conclusions at the time. The mayor reviewed the photos of the four other girls and read their different backgrounds. The third page contained the police report on the case.

According to the report, in Laketown, Virginia, five college seniors were reported missing. After extensive investigations—interviewing family members, friends, and professors—it became clear that these five friends and sorority sisters had been abducted and killed, possibly by the same perpetrator or group.

The bodies of four victims were later found deep in the woods, with no fingerprints or evidence left behind. Evelyn Bridges' family reported that her body had been found separately and buried the same day. The killer was never found. The lead detective on the case was Charles Lee.

After reviewing the file in silence for nearly ten minutes, the mayor slowly reached for her leather briefcase and handed Cheryl a new file. Just then, Delilah returned with Cheryl's breakfast sandwich and a glass of water.

"Would you like anything else?"

"No, thank you. And thank you for the water—that was very considerate," Cheryl said appreciatively.

"You're welcome, ma'am. I'll check on you both in a few," Delilah said.

"Thank you again, Delilah," the mayor added.

"Anytime, Mayor Goodman. Mama said you're family. Just holler if you need anything," Delilah said as she walked away.

Cheryl was about to take a bite of her sandwich when the mayor interrupted.

"So, based on this information, Elaine Blake—formerly Evelyn Bridges—was from Old Laketown. She was the daughter of Robert and Violet Bridges and the great-granddaughter of Robert Bridges, one of Laketown's original founders."

"That's correct. But why did she lie to her daughter all these years and leave her family behind?" the mayor asked, perplexed.

"I'm guessing because she was supposed to be dead. That's the only reason I can think of," Cheryl mumbled, finally taking a bite.

"It's crazy—I remember how devastated her brother and sister were at the funeral, but her mother barely cried. At least, I didn't see her."

"I know this happened twenty years ago, but have you spoken to the lead detective at the time? Charles Lee?" the mayor asked.

"Charles Lee was my father. He followed in the footsteps of his father and grandfather as one of Laketown's first Black lawmen. But he died while pursuing the killer. His body was found deep in the woods days before Evelyn's family reported finding hers. They refused to have an open casket at his funeral," Cheryl said solemnly.

The mayor's face softened. "Oh, I'm so sorry for your loss."

"Thank you. But I won't rest until the truth is revealed. My intuition tells me that this case will uncover the answers we both need," Cheryl said, finishing her breakfast.

CHAPTER FIVE

WASHINGTON

CHAPTER FIVE
Washington

Wendell walked out of the bar, his black hood pulled over his head, and scanned the lot for Lloyd's truck. The all-black SUV was parked at the end of the lot. Wendell had found an empty spot right next to it, which was perfect—he didn't want to make a scene. With so much happening in this small town, he had no idea who might be watching.

It was late at night. A few couples walked past him, too caught up in their own drunken laughter to notice him. They looked like this bar was their second or third stop of the night, already tipsy from the last one. Wendell moved as quietly as possible toward his burgundy Tahoe, which had plenty of space in the back. Definitely enough room for a body.

Sliding into his truck, he backed up next to Lloyd's all-black Cadillac Escalade—definitely something a Black doctor would drive. He pulled out Lloyd's keys, which he had taken after drugging the man at the table. Lloyd hadn't even noticed. Quickly, Wendell unlocked the trunk, lifted the body, and carefully placed it inside his own truck. Then he shut the trunk of the Escalade and left Lloyd's keys on the dashboard in plain sight.

If someone came along and stole the good doctor's truck, Wendell couldn't care less. But in this small town, he doubted Lloyd had anything to worry about.

He had unfinished business to clean up before making one more stop—his aunt's house. Aunt Anna had always kept an eye on everything for Wendell. She had been his guardian angel while she was alive. Ever since his mother's tragic death, Aunt Anna—his mother's older sister—had felt responsible for him. She had known he was a strange child, but she had also recognized his intelligence.

He had brought a brand-new brochure for Laketown University. It was for a special someone. If everything went according to plan, she would be closer to him within weeks. He had worked too hard over the years, meticulously planning every detail. She had tried so hard to create a false world for herself, but in the end, Wendell would take it all from her—just like her family had taken everything from him.

Being back in McDillion, Georgia, brought back so many memories of his mother and his favorite aunt. Aunt Anna had lived just outside of town, enjoying her peace and quiet. After Uncle Wilbert died, she had been lonely, but the timing had worked out perfectly. She had been out of the loop for so long, but when she answered Wendell's call and heard his plan, she had easily played her part. She had even grown to like Evelyn, which had surprised Wendell. He hadn't thought she would stay as long as she had, but whatever. It had all worked out. Even after Aunt Anna's death, everything was still moving in the right direction.

After hours of driving, Wendell finally made it back, taking a detour to avoid the main highways and traffic lights of Laketown. He passed the campus of his alma mater, Laketown University, taking the back roads before crossing the old Laketown bridge into the community.

Even though his life had been dark for years, he had always loved his community. There was no place like it. Being born and raised in Old Laketown was something he would always be proud of. But that pride would never outweigh the pain this community had caused him and his family. People always said time heals all wounds, but Wendell disagreed. Time didn't heal anything. For him, revenge was the only thing that could make the pain go away.

Revenge for the suffering they had caused. Revenge for the years they had stolen from him. Revenge for the life of the most important person in his world—his mother.

He remembered how his mother used to take him on walks down Old Laketown Road, visiting the shops and dancing to the music played by the local quartets in the street. But with the anniversary of her death approaching, this same community only reminded him of how rotten even his own people could be.

She would be avenged. They would never get away with what they had allowed to happen to his mother.

1960: The Rise of Laketown

In 1960, Laketown experienced an industrial boom. New buildings were being constructed, and large corporations brought factories and thousands of manufacturing jobs with them. In just a short time, Laketown's population skyrocketed from the hundreds to the thousands.

The Black-owned businesses in Old Laketown were thriving. The schools—built and run by Black educators—were outperforming some of the highest-ranked schools in the country. Laketown University saw a surge in admissions, with its programs achieving great success. Though it had only been about ten years since schools were forced to integrate, the student body had chosen to remain informally segregated—Black students on one side of campus, white students on the other.

Community leaders in Old Laketown raised money to expand the university's campus housing, maintaining the neighborhood's signature Victorian architecture. They also built a prestigious cafeteria, staffed with their own chefs, a full kitchen, and an onsite garden.

Shirley White was a young, single mother who worked in the cafeteria as an assistant to the new head chef. She helped harvest fresh fruits and vegetables from the garden and prepared them for the lunch and dinner menus. Many of the female cooks worked long hours but lived off-campus, across the bridge.

Because of the university's growing success, the dean and board decided to hold the first L.U. Banquet, hoping to unite the student body through departmental showcases.

The day of the banquet, Shirley's son fell ill at school, forcing her to leave her shift. She asked her coworkers to cover for her and promised to return for the night shift to help prepare dinner for the banquet.

The celebration started off well, but as the night progressed, a fight broke out over inappropriate touching. The banquet hall was quickly trashed by drunken students who refused to leave. Their rowdiness spilled outside, causing havoc on campus.

When Shirley returned, she brought her son with her, instructing him to sit quietly in the back of the kitchen while she cleaned up. Taking the trash out to the alley, she was met by a group of drunken white fraternity brothers. They pulled on her clothes and pushed her around. When she screamed, her son ran to the door—only to witness the horrific scene unfold before him.

Five different men attacked his mother, beating her unconscious before taking turns violating her. He screamed for them to stop, but they wouldn't listen. When he ran out to fight them off, one of them grabbed his head and slammed it against the brick wall. His right eye struck the brick, and he lost consciousness.

Hours later, Black faculty members found them both.

The incident was reported to Old Laketown's leadership and the university administration. Days later, Shirley's husband met with both groups. To protect the new city's prosperity, the university's reputation, and Old Laketown's future, a decision was made.

A settlement.

Shirley's husband accepted $500,000 in hush money. Justice was never served.

Months later, Shirley awoke from a coma—but she was never the same. Her son, traumatized, spent his free time at her bedside. But because of her deteriorating mental state, he was forced to move in with his father.

Days later, Shirley slit her wrists and bled out in her bathtub.

After her burial, her husband purchased a large plot of land deep in the woods on the outskirts of Old Laketown and built a massive mountain cabin. He remarried a beautiful young woman, Mariana Turner, and started Washington Builders & Landscaping, a business that became a major success in Old Laketown.

Mariana was connected to one of Old Laketown's founding families. She embraced her ancestral spiritual practices and immediately sensed the darkness inside Shirley's son—Wendell, Jr.

She taught him about biology, bloodwork, and the dark arts. She shared her knowledge of the human body and science.

She became Wendell's favorite person.

But nothing—not even Mariana—could make him forget his first love.

His mother.

And what they did to her.

Wendell vs Cain

By the age of seven, Wendell began displaying behaviors that deeply concerned his parents. At first, his problems surfaced at school. His teacher complained that he was bullying a couple of his classmates.

In the mornings, he was kind—offering to share his pencils with friends. But after lunch, he would push those same classmates around, claiming he had never given them any pencils and threatening to bust their lips if they didn't return them.

At home, after playing in the woods, Wendell would find small animals to keep as pets. Later, his stepmother would stumble upon their lifeless corpses in the basement, blood dripping from their tiny bodies. Whenever his parents confronted him about it, Wendell would look utterly confused.

"I don't know what happened," he would say, tears welling up in his young eyes. "It wasn't me. I didn't kill my birdie. I didn't slit the squirrel's throat."

His parents felt terrible for him, believing the trauma he had endured at such an early age was to blame. But the darkness continued, creeping in and out of his behavior like a shadow he couldn't escape.

This pattern continued off and on for another year. Then, one night, everything reached a terrifying turning point.

The Restroom Incident

It was late. Marianna was shutting the house down for the night when she heard an eerie voice coming from the hallway. She paused, listening. Slowly, she climbed the stairs, each step bringing her closer to the unsettling sounds.

When she reached the hallway, she stopped. Two voices were coming from inside the restroom. Her heart pounded. One voice belonged to Wendell, a young, innocent eight-year-old boy. The other…The other sounded monstrous. A deep, menacing voice—something dark, something unnatural.

Marianna froze outside the bathroom door, straining to hear, fear gripping her.

"Please," Wendell's voice pleaded. "I can't do it. I can't keep killing God's precious animals. He loves them."

"Stop being so weak," the other voice sneered. "Just snap his neck and slice him right down the middle."

"Please don't do this," Wendell begged. "Dad is gonna find out, and we might get in trouble."

"Do it, you weak, pathetic little boy. No one cares about you. God hates you and your dead mother. Kill the squirrel, or I will kill them."

"No, no! Don't you hurt them! Fine… if this is what you want."

Suddenly, Marianna heard a horrible, high-pitched screech. The helpless baby squirrel's cries were cut short by the sharp slice of a knife. Then the faucet turned on. Cleaning up the mess. Marianna shrank into a dark corner, holding her breath.

Moments later, Wendell emerged, carrying the dead squirrel wrapped in a towel. She waited until he was gone, then rushed into the restroom. No one was there. Only Wendell.

The next morning, Marianna took Wendell to the town pediatrician. She sat in his office, hands clenched, recounting the disturbing events. "Something's wrong with him," she admitted. "I think he needs help."

The doctor spent time speaking with Wendell before running psychiatric evaluations. After reviewing the results, he called both parents into the room.

"I believe Wendell may have a serious mental disorder," he explained gently. "I recommend further testing. And… medication."

But Wendell Sr. wasn't having it. He slammed his fist on the doctor's desk. "My son doesn't need to be doped up on medicine," he declared. "The good Lord will heal him in time. He just needs love. His family. And maybe the church."

That same day, Wendell Sr. made a decision. The Washington family joined the Temple of God Anointed, led by the Holy Bishop Marianna hoped it would be enough.

But deep down…She knew it wouldn't be.

THE BRIDGES

CHAPTER SIX
The Bridges

Violet

A tall, slender woman with fine gray hair brushed back into a single, neat braid that hung past her shoulders and rested in the middle of her back stood peering through the open windows of her study. Inhaling the fresh evening air, she sensed a shift within her spirit, though she couldn't quite put her finger on it.

Ever since Saturday night, her sleep had been off. Nightmares came continuously, and restless nights stretched into the last few days. She knew something was wrong—or maybe she was just overreacting.

As she enjoyed the view, she caught sight of her herbalist, Mary Woods, walking along the sidewalk, pushing her small cart of fresh herbs back home across the Old Laketown Bridge. Seeing her friend again brought relief. She hadn't seen Mary in a while, and mutual friends had spoken of her failing health.

Stepping onto the grand front porch, Violet waved over the shrubs along the metal fence, greeting her with a smile.

"Well, hello there, stranger! It's so nice to see you out this evening."

"Hello, Violet. It's nice to be seen these days."

"How have you been, Mary? I heard you were under the weather. I was concerned and prayed for your healing. And look at you now, up and about, back to doing what you love—healing us all with your precious gifts."

"Oh, Violet Bridges if you were praying for me, I know God had to answer. There's nothing like having a prayer warrior on your side."

"You better believe it, Mary. I'm always looking out for my ladies in the community. Now, let's see what you have left on your cart. I'd love to lighten your load."

"Well, thank you, but all I have left from today's market is fresh collards, parsley, and freshly picked dandelions—grown only from my ancestral garden, passed down from five generations of Woods Women," Mary said, her voice tinged with pride.

"Oh yes, Mary, let me take all of that off your hands, honey," Violet said, rubbing her hands together with excitement. "I have great recipes for each one, and I've been running low on collards since the last time I saw you."

"Great, just send me the usual payment tomorrow, and I'll see you next time. There's an eerie wind blowing tonight, and I believe it's because of the blood moon that's coming," Mary said, looking up at the night sky.

Her intuition was always sharp, a power that aided her ancestral gifts. Being a Woods Woman, a healer of the land, came with wisdom and deep knowing.

Violet trusted Mary's words. Throughout the years, she had always been right about the weather, the seasons, and every plant grown from Mother Earth.

"You know, I was standing in my study, feeling the breeze, and I had an uneasy feeling in my spirit. I wonder if that has anything to do with it," Violet said, looking in Mary's direction.

"This moon ain't just any moon. This harvest season brings forth the blood harvest moon. We haven't had one in over twenty years. They always come with a sacrifice."

Violet didn't respond.

She was frozen in place.

Her face twisted into something unrecognizable—an expression of deep-seated fear as if every nightmare she had ever buried was suddenly coming back to life.

"Dear God, Violet, are you okay?" Mary asked, concern laced in her voice. "Mrs. Bridges, you look like you've seen a ghost. Even your skin is cold to the touch. Should I call for help?"

"No… No, Mary, I'm fine. I just need to sit on the porch and rest. Thank you so much, my friend, for the fresh greens. I'll have someone bring your payment in the morning."

"Okay, I'm gonna get a little exercise and head on back. My Cheryl is out of town, so it's just me at the house, but I'll see you soon. Take good care now."

"Yes, love, you do the same."

"Oh yes, ma'am, I definitely will."

Cassy

Walking into the grand foyer of her childhood home, Cassandra Bridges called for her mother but got no response.

Her hands were full of colorful decorations she had pulled down from the attic at her mother's request. Since her divorce after ten years of marriage, she had moved back home. Her mother's health was in slow decline, and she knew they needed each other.

Though a small staff still remained to help maintain the family estate, Cassandra missed being here—missed being close to her mother. She assumed she would find her in the family study, where she often read and communed with their ancestors. But when she turned to the open window, she was surprised to see her mother outside, standing by the front gate, talking to Mary Woods. A smile spread across Cassandra's face. She knew she would be eating well later.

Her mother was known for her smoked turkey necks and collard greens. And Miss Woods always had the freshest vegetables and herbs at the local markets. She sold out often but always saved some for Violet because of their long-standing friendship.

A cool autumn breeze drifted into the family study, causing Cassandra to close the windows. She loved the season but wasn't excited about the cold that would soon follow. Seeing the two older women still chatting along the sidewalk, she decided to mind her business and wait for her mother's instructions. She set the decorations down and called for Mason, their loyal servant and close family friend, to help place them in the different rooms.

Outside of her mother, Mason was the only one who knew exactly what needed to go where and how it should look. If it weren't for Mason, Cassandra was sure her mother would have lost her mind a long time ago.

Just then, the house phone in the library rang, grabbing Cassandra's attention. She glanced toward her mother. In a swift motion, she decided to answer.

"Hello," she said in a calm, soothing tone.

"Hello, this is the office of Mayor Gladys Goodman of McDillion, Georgia calling to speak with Cassandra Bridges. Is she available?" the secretary asked.

Cassandra's brows furrowed.

"Um, yes, this is Cassandra Bridges. How can I help you?"

"Please hold for the mayor. I'll transfer you now."

"The mayor? Oh… okay, thank you."

A moment later, a new voice came through the receiver—one filled with authority and confidence.

"Hello, Cassandra Bridges, I presume."

"Yes, this is she. And why do I have the pleasure of speaking with the mayor of McDillion, Georgia, this evening?" Cassandra asked, suspicion laced in her voice.

"Well, Miss Bridges, I'm sorry to say that I'm not reaching out with the best news. Are you sitting down?"

Cassandra sat up straight in the plush, black-and-gold-trimmed Cappelletti Royal swivel office chair, suddenly intrigued.

"Well, actually, I am sitting at my family study desk, Mayor Goodman. What is this news you are sorry to share?"

"Miss Bridges, typically, I'd have the sheriff's department handle this, but I decided to make this call personally due to the sensitivity of the situation. After conducting some research, I believe you may be able to help me with this case."

"Case? What case?" Cassandra gasped.

"Did you know anyone by the name of Elaine Blake? We have reason to believe she was from your area or possibly even a daughter of Old Laketown—maybe from one of the original families."

The silence that followed was so thick it was almost suffocating.

The mayor nearly questioned whether Cassandra had heard her at all. Then, finally—

"Elaine Blake?" "Yes. Do you recognize the name?"

Cassandra hesitated.

"I'm so sorry, but I don't know an Elaine Blake. I don't recognize that family name either. Are you sure your research shows her being from this area in Virginia?"

"Yes, but I was told she had no family and relocated to McDillion about twenty years ago. However, after reviewing her records, the coroner's office confirmed she was originally from your area and possibly from your family."

Shock ran up Cassandra's spine. She had no idea what this woman was talking about. She had no family outside of Old Laketown.

"Miss Bridges, is it possible for you to come to McDillion soon? I know this might sound crazy right now, but as I mentioned before, this is a very special case. I really could use your help, if you're willing," Mayor Goodman asked, her tone sincere.

Cassandra hesitated but remained professional. "I understand. And from my research, you work for Old Laketown University, correct?"

"Yes," Cassandra confirmed. "I am the Head of Admissions. My family is one of the original families that established the prestigious university over 150 years ago. It's very important to us and our community."

"Exactly. And we have reason to believe that the murder victim, Elaine Blake, may have been a student at OLU twenty years ago."

"Twenty years ago?" Cassandra echoed, sitting up in her chair. "I'll have to look into the school's database for more information. If she was a student, there may be records that can help. I might also remember more about a missing girl from that time."

A pause.

"When and where can we meet, Mayor Goodman? I am very interested in this case, especially if this Blake woman was an OLU alum," Cassandra expressed.

"Oh, thank you so much, Miss Bridges. I'm sorry to bother you so late this evening, but I made a promise to someone very special to me that I would do everything in my power to help Elaine Blake's daughter." The mayor's voice softened. "She's almost eighteen. Now abandoned. No family.

And as a mother myself, my intuition tells me something isn't right about it."

Cassandra exhaled sharply. "Oh my God, a daughter? Alone with no family?"

Her heart clenched. It was a tragic, unfortunate reality—especially if this young girl was a possible descendant of the original families.

"I actually have this weekend off because of OLU's Fall Festival," Cassandra offered. "Let's meet Friday morning and discuss Elaine Blake's case. We can also talk about how my family might be able to help her daughter."

"Thank you, Miss Bridges. Please meet me at Miss Dee's Diner this Friday morning at ten a.m."

"Okay, got it. And, Mayor Goodman—please, my friends call me Cassy."

"Thank you. I'll do the same. See you Friday, Cassy."

"See you then, Mayor."

The Wickum House

I couldn't sleep at all last night. It was like my mind refused to turn off. So much had been said about my mother, and my brain struggled to put things in their place. Tossing and turning throughout the night left me feeling delirious. Waking up to silence is a part of grief I had never known. There are real levels to this nightmare reality I'm living. With my eyes closed, I imagine my soul as a large stone resting on the shore of the ocean while the strong tide of grief drowns me more and more each day. But it never lifts me or lightens my load, just constantly crashes into me from every direction, breaking me down bit by bit.

With every breath I take, I exhale surrender. I surrender to the pain and the loss of my mother. I surrender to the hurt of silence and emptiness that surrounds me everywhere I go. I thought about leaving the house today, but every place I turn, in every direction I look, all I see is her. McDillion, Georgia is her. She is everywhere for me in this town. I can't move from my bed. My body is still, full of emotions that can't be expressed. My throat is dry and cramps with every thought of her not coming home. My eyes are bloodshot red, my eyelids swollen like pillows, moving sluggishly whenever I force them to participate with the rest of my body. Eventually, my need to relieve myself forces me out of bed. Slowly, I rise and walk into the hallway at about four a.m.—the time I usually wake up for the restroom anyway.

Coming out of the dark, avoiding all mirrors and light for the sake of my own disappointment, I see something. Light. A glow creeping from underneath Mama's bedroom door. In an instant, the sweet young girl within me—the one I thought had died at the memorial—rushes forward with high hopes. Maybe they made a mistake. Maybe she isn't dead. Maybe I will wake up from this nightmare with my mother looking me in the eyes, asking if I'm okay. Maybe the mayor and the sheriff had it all wrong. Maybe it was another Elaine, the one with family originally from Virginia. But when I open the door, no one is there. Only the room. And the full moon, illuminating every aspect of her world.

Her Estée Lauder perfume, filled with sweet yet robust scents of rose, lily, and citrus, lingers in the air, warming my heart. Taut with emotion, my body stiffens, absorbing the cruel truth. Why? Why you, Mama? Why us? You were so young. So healthy. Why did this have to happen to us? What am I supposed to do now? Wiping the tears from my face, I notice something. The full moon shines its brightest on Mama's old trunk, sitting next to her vanity. A warmth fills the air. A sensation I can't explain. Startled, I reach out. The moment my fingers brush the handle, the warmth intensifies. My hands tremble as I lift the lid.

Inside, old nightgowns, t-shirts, and linens are neatly folded. But beneath them, something solid. Something the size of a history book. It comes to life under the moonlight—a book, ancient and magnificent. The base is pure black, its golden carvings intricate and hypnotic. A fixed sculpture adorns the front—a black woman, carved from smooth obsidian stone. Her regal face, calm and knowing, is framed by flowing locs that merge into a crescent moon. Under the moon's glow, she looks… familiar. Like Mama. But that isn't possible. This book is ancient. I had never seen anything like it. A relic from a world beyond mine.

I sat down in the vanity chair, setting the book on the wooden table. A flash of heat rushed through my body, warming my cheeks. With unsteady hands, I flipped open the first page. "*Dedicated to the Daughters of the Great Mother.*" A handwritten note was tucked inside. "This book is a gift for my daughter, Ebony. Happy Eighteenth!" My mother's handwriting. My heart stopped. This was the surprise gift she had mentioned. She knew I would have loved it. She knew. Tears blurred my vision. As I continued reading, the words burned red like fire, as if alive. This wasn't just a book. It was a sacred collection—a lineage of journals written by women dating back to the early 1800s. And at the very end—Mama's section. I couldn't turn away. I missed her too much. I needed to hear her voice, even if only through the pages.

June 13, 1980. I am so humbled to be writing in this sacred book. For so long, I have wanted to be special, to be the chosen one for something. I always assumed it would be Cassy. She is the oldest, the favorite child of my mother. But I think everyone was shocked when my name was called to be the next Divine Daughter of the family. After reading the writings of my ancestors and their journeys on this righteous path, I am ready to learn the ways of the Divine Daughters and wear our ancient obsidian stone cross on my chest. The stone of blood, given to us by the dark angel who blessed the Great Mother Mary. It will enhance the blood of my foremothers that runs through my veins. Even though I don't know exactly what my role will be, I know that I will do everything I can to make my mothers proud. One day, when I have a daughter of my own, I will be able to pass down this sacred honor to her. I exhale deeply. My body trembles as I turn the page. I don't know if I am ready for this, but I continue.

July 10, 1980. I met the most perfect young man today. He was in the biology building, and I saw him as we both walked into anatomy class. It was weird because I think he knew me—or at least, he acted like he did. But I had never seen him before in my life. He spoke my name and smiled when he let me enter the doorway first, a gentleman. His skin was a deep, smooth rich brown, which complemented his strong jawline and high cheekbones. But his eyes... His eyes were the most telling. They were black, almond-shaped, with a deep scar that cut sharply down beside his right eye. I had never seen eyes like his before. The scar was a stark, jagged line, slightly raised and darker than the surrounding skin. It disrupted his otherwise symmetrical, strikingly handsome face. Even though we sat on different ends of the room, I could not stop looking at him, subtly searching to see if he was staring back. I was. And he did.

I shivered. Who was she talking about? My pulse quickened as I flipped through more entries, searching for answers. But as I read further, something felt… off. My mother's words became more frantic, uncertain. A sense of unease washed over me. She was scared.

September 21, 1980. It has been two whole months since we first met, and I feel like we can't stop feeding off of each other. I love being in his presence, but I think something is wrong. At first, I thought it was just me. But now I know the truth. It's not me. It's him. And whatever he is doing to me.

My heart pounded in my chest. I slammed the book shut, unable to read further. I needed answers. I needed to know who my mother was writing about. I needed to know what she was afraid of. And more than anything, I needed to know why she never told me.

Anna Wickum

In a hypnotic sleep, deep yet weightless, I felt my body being lifted from the bed, bathed in the glow of the moon. With my eyes closed, I sensed a dark figure—black as the night's shadow—with piercing red eyes watching and waiting near the closet in the far corner of the room. Then, a mysterious locked door appeared. Frightened, I tried to open my eyes, to move my body, but nothing worked. I was frozen, trapped within myself, yet I could feel its power drawing closer.

Who is this? What do they want with me? What is happening to me? Why can't I move? Every instinct in me screamed to run, but I was helpless. I was no longer in control of my own body. With slow, calculated steps, the dark figure approached, its presence eerily familiar. Then, suddenly, a glowing sphere—shimmering like the moon—appeared around me, shielding me from its touch. The atmosphere trembled from within the moonlit sphere, shaking like an earthquake each time the dark spirit tried to break through. Then, a loud inner voice spoke: *It's in your blood.*

The cool fall breeze brushed against the window blinds, creating a tapping sound that slowly pulled me out of what felt like a deep and heavy sleep. My eyes opened abruptly, dazed and terrified. I lay still, my mind racing, questioning what had just happened and what it had to do with the book my mother had left me. Turning my head, I saw the book still open to my mother's journal section—but the pictures were gone. Maybe I dropped them, or they had fallen out of the bed while I was asleep. Determined to find them, I searched everywhere—under the bed, beneath the pillows and comforter—but there was no sign of them.

A flash of my dream rushed back, and my thoughts fixated on Mama's closet and that locked door. But Mama's closet never had a locked door. I had never seen anything like that in her room before. It was just a dream... wasn't it? My curiosity got the best of me. I needed to check. As I stepped closer to the far side of the bedroom, an unsettling sensation crept up my spine. Goosebumps rose on my arms. My hands trembled as I reached for the closet door and opened it. Inside, her clothes hung neatly, her shoes aligned perfectly on the floor, and shoe boxes were stacked on the top shelf.

Moving her clothes aside, I reached up to search further, and a loose box tumbled to the floor. The lid popped open, and its contents spilled out—mail, all addressed to *Anna Wickum.* My heart pounded as I stared at the name. Again, more things that belonged to Anna Wickum. Who was this woman? And why did my mother have all her mail hidden away in her closet? This was crazy.

Sorting through the first box, I pulled out a handful of envelopes, their dates stretching back to the 1990s. There were electric bills, medical bills from McDillion Hospital, and letters from the McDillion Baptist Church, addressed to *Mrs. Wickum* from *Pastor Johnson.* These boxes were filled with everyday mail for Anna Wickum—nothing particularly special. So why hadn't Mama just thrown them away?

Then, it hit me.

A sharp, painful realization settled deep in my chest, in that place where pain and betrayal coexist. My eyes opened to a truth I hadn't been ready to see, but now, I couldn't ignore it. She had been *hiding it from me*.

The little girl who worshipped her mother had died at her memorial.

Confusion twisted into anger. All the subtle changes I had noticed throughout my childhood started to peel away, revealing something I had never dared to question. Tears slipped from my eyes. I didn't deserve this. I had been a good daughter. *God, I did not deserve this.* My anger, once buried, was starting to rise—not just at my mother but at *God himself*.

I needed answers.

I needed to talk to someone—someone who could help me make sense of this darkness that was growing inside me.

Then, as if fate had placed it right at my feet, I noticed a letter resting just beside my foot. It was addressed to *Anna Wickum* from the church.

I bent down, picked it up, and turned it over in my hands.

Maybe this was a sign.

Maybe it was time to go see the pastor.

MCDILLION BAPTIST

CHAPTER SEVEN
McDillion Baptist

McDillion is a small town full of longleaf pine trees that can grow up to a hundred feet in height. The pines are old, way older than me or anything that I know. I'm sure these ancient beings have seen it all through their thousand years of existence. Walking through, I imagine they've witnessed every storm, every fire, and even the people who came and went. Bodies planted in the same soil that their roots are so deeply established in. When I think about it in that way, we are connected to them, whether we like it or not.

From the house, I can get to everything. It's kind of located on the outskirts of town. Depending on where I'm walking or riding my bike, I can take different routes to reach various parts of McDillion. If I turn right, I'll head toward McDillion High School, the library, and Dillion Lake. If I turn left, I'll find myself in town, where there's shopping, local diners, and big chain restaurants. But if I go straight across, I pass through the forest of towering longleaf pines, down a long road leading straight to the church and the McDillion cemetery. Beyond the cemetery, the Dillion Lake curves and flows, a peaceful place where people go to take in the serene views and breathe in the fresh scent of Georgia pines.

The old Southern Baptist church stands tall, newly renovated with fresh white paint on the upper half and tan-colored stone bricks leading down to the walking pathways. The steeple points toward the sky, sharp and sure, as if reaching out to God himself. The church windows are large and arched, their stained glass glowing softly under the high sun. The ten-foot-tall solid pinewood doors are heavy and dark, commanding attention from all who approach. As I walk up slowly, I think of my mother and how much she loved the sweet, heavy scent of magnolias mixed with wood and freshly cut grass. The church's front courtyard, decorated with vibrant flowers and fragrant trees, was the work of Mrs. Johnson, the pastor's wife. She owns two floral shops in town and provides arrangements for the church and the funeral home just down the street.

When I push open the church doors, they make a deep groaning sound. Though empty, the quiet church feels alive, as if the walls have absorbed all the hymns sung and prayers whispered throughout the years. My breathing feels loud against the stillness of the sanctuary. The scent of old hymnals and polished pews washes over me as I walk closer to the altar and quietly settle behind Pastor Johnson as he prays.

"Ebony Blake, I was just lifting you and so many others up to the Lord this afternoon. And now, I lift my eyes to see you sitting right behind me," he says in surprise. "I tell you, God works in mysterious ways."

"How have you been these last couple of days?" he asks with concern.

"Not my best, Pastor Johnson, but I'm trying more and more every day to understand. I'm either really sad and confused about things or really angry. I blame my mother, and I blame God for this nightmare reality that I'm living," I say, tears swelling in my eyes as tension rises in my throat.

"Wait a minute, child. I know everything feels overwhelming, but you can't blame God. He's the one you should be clinging to. He'll give you understanding and shine His light of clarity when everything seems dark."

"But Pastor, He's also the one who took my mother from me. At one of the worst times in my life. I should be getting ready for college, packing up for freshman year in a university somewhere. But no, I'm home alone and abandoned. And on top of all of that, I'm learning things about my own mother that I never even knew," I say, frustration thick in my voice.

"Come, child. Let's talk in my office," he says, glancing around as if searching for listening ears before leading me down a back hallway lit by fancy brass lanterns, a new addition to the old church building.

As I step into the pastor's private quarters, I'm taken aback. It's more than I expected—like stepping into a different world or maybe a different time. My senses heighten, my thoughts grow sharper. The cross on my chest warms against my skin, just like it did last night beneath the moonlight. The room carries an air of quiet authority, almost regal. The walls are framed in warm dark wood, lined with shelves filled with worn, leather-bound books—volumes of wisdom, history, sermons, and theological studies. The decor is elegantly Victorian, the soft glow of brass lanterns casting a gentle light across the space.

The rich black and gold fibers of the large rug, accented with hints of deep red, perfectly complement the grand desk and the luxurious black leather chair with gold trim that anchors the center of the room. The heavy aroma of fresh magnolias drifts from a large bouquet placed by the window, where thick drapes frame the glass. Beside the window hangs a cross, and below it, an eight-by-ten framed portrait of a man holding a Bible and a cross in his hands. Around his neck hangs a small black and gold medallion shaped like a crescent moon—the same symbol from the book I found in my mother's trunk.

I walk directly to the portrait, drawn to the necklace and the man wearing it.

"The Holy Bishop," Pastor Johnson announces, surprised by my sudden interest.

"This is a beautiful portrait of him. For some reason, I feel like I've seen him before. Has he been to the church recently, Pastor?" I ask, trying to place his face.

"Oh, he doesn't do much traveling now that he's up in age. But his son will soon take his place. He too is a powerful man of God," the pastor replies.

"Pastor Johnson, what is that on his neck?" I ask.

He walks over, studying the image.

"Well, that is an old symbol representing our power and influence on this planet. You see, there's nothing new under the sun. For Black people in this country, we had to take our freedom—to live, to pray, to believe. This moon is a representation of that in the Black Christian community."

The pastor gestures for me to sit in one of two black leather chairs placed atop the soft fiber rug. The chairs are positioned perfectly across from his desk, creating an intimate space for conversation.

"Pastor Johnson, it's beautiful here. I've never seen such class. And those fresh magnolias make the whole room smell amazing," I say in awe.

"Well, thank you, Ebony. These are my private quarters where I meditate on God's word, research, and write my sermons," he says with pride.

"You know, I come from a long line of spiritual leaders. It's literally in my blood," he chuckles.

"Did my mama ever come to see you here?" I ask, my curiosity growing.

"Oh yes, I remember seeing her more when she was younger, less as she got older. She was a firecracker."

I smile in agreement, but sadness lingers in my eyes. Pastor Johnson reaches out his hands—warm, dark, strong. His left hand bears a gold wedding band, his right a striking black onyx stone set in a solid gold band.

"Ebony, you are a young lady now, and unfortunately, you've been forced to grow up much faster than others at this time in your life. But that doesn't mean you have to lose faith in God."

"Pastor Johnson, I haven't lost faith, but I am losing trust. Trust in my mother, in the woman I thought she was. Trust in God because He allows this. If He loves us so much, why does He allow bad things to happen to the innocent?"

"I believe, based on scripture and stories from the Bible, that He allows us to be tested so that His glory is revealed in our lives. Just like Job. Job was tested but still gave God the glory, and he was restored with more than he had before."

"Young lady, maybe this is your test from God. What is He revealing to you?" he asks, looking deep into my soul.

Before I can answer, the phone rings.

"Excuse me a moment, Ms. Blake," he says, stepping away.

As he speaks, I wander the room, taking in old photos of the church, its original members from 1975, the pastor as a young man, and an elegant collage of important Black men and women who favor him in different ways. Then I remember the name—*Anna Wickum*. I turn back to the pastor, determined to ask him about her.

To give him privacy, I continue my personal tour of his quarters. The walls behind us are filled with more pictures—historic photos, including one of the church, and its founding members, encased with the date 1975. There are photos of the pastor as a young man and another of him and his wife. In an elegant collage, separate portraits of distinguished Black men and women are displayed, all favoring the pastor in some way.

"Yes, of course. I'll be there this afternoon. No worries. You're welcome. Goodbye," he says, ending his call.

"I'm so sorry, Ebony, but we're going to have to cut this visit short. You know, a pastor's work is never done. But was there anything else I could help you with before we pray?"

"Yes, Pastor, there is. Can you tell me who Anna Wickum is? I found a lot of her mail in my mother's things, and I'm confused. Who is she, and why did my mother never tell me about her?"

"Well, young Ebony, Mrs. Anna Mae Wickum was the owner of the house you were raised in, the very house you wake up in every morning. Anna Mae left it to your mother and you when she passed."

"But was she related to us or something? I just don't understand why she would leave her house to us for nothing," I reply, my confusion deepening.

Pastor Johnson looks up at me with a hint of pity in his eyes—something he quickly tries to brush off by rustling papers on his desk.

"Pastor Johnson, there's something you're not telling me, sir. Because I know that look. My mama had that same look when she was hiding something," I say, leaning slightly in his direction.

"I think your mother believed she was protecting you by keeping you in the dark. Even though I advised her not to, she was a firecracker—very stubborn when it came to you."

"So, you spoke to her about it? When? Why did she never say anything to me?"

"Ebony, the first time I laid eyes on your mother was twenty years ago. She was Anna Mae's watch nurse. They call them hospice nurses now, but when I was a boy, Black folks called them watch nurses. They watched over souls in transition."

"Yeah, she did have a soft spot for old people," I say with a small smile. "But what does that have to do with us living in Ms. Wickum's house?"

"Honey, Anna Mae loved your mother. She was the daughter she wished she had. When she found out your mother was pregnant and that her cancer had gotten worse, she had it written in her will that her home and assets would belong to Elaine Blake and her child," he says, then looks at me. "You know, your mother had a beautiful headstone and plot made for Mrs. Wickum right in the McDillion cemetery. Now that you know about Miss Anna Mae, you should go by and pay your respects. It might help give you some comfort during this difficult time.

"Miss Anna set it up for you, so technically, when you turn eighteen, the house, the land, and all her belongings will be yours. Your name is already on it, but the rights will be transferred after your eighteenth birthday."

The pastor has another family in distress waiting for him, so I thank him for his time. I've learned a lot from our talk, but I can't shake the feeling that he knows more. Maybe my mother told him not to tell me. Or maybe… I just don't know anymore.

The Case

The walk back to the house felt different. On my way to the church, my mind was filled with thoughts of the forest and its splendor, but on my way back, my thoughts took a completely different turn. I decided to listen to Pastor Johnson's advice and walk down the long-cemented path from the church to the historic McDillion Cemetery.

One thing about First Lady Johnson—her floral touch is everywhere in McDillion's Black community. The trees and floral landscaping along the path brought a sense of peace, almost as if they were comforting me along my walk. The cemetery itself was calm, quiet. Unlike a few days ago at Mama's memorial, I was now able to take in the beauty and care put into this place. You could tell that the town took pride in this resting ground. The tombstones were displayed neatly, some dating back to the 1800s.

After passing through the older sections, I finally came across the Wickums. Wilbert Wickum's tombstone was old and weathered, its lettering slowly fading with time, but Anna Mae Wickum's was newer, much larger, and well cared for. I don't know how much Mama spent, but she chose a beautiful display. The tombstone had a framed picture of Miss Anna and a heartfelt message etched below: *May God keep your soul safe in His arms, until we meet again.*

I had never owned anything in my life, outside of what my mama bought for me. I had no idea I was a homeowner. I had no idea of the gift that was given to me by a woman I had never met, yet who loved me enough to think of my future.

Anna Mae Wickum looked out for Mama and me. Out of the kindness of her heart, she gave us something priceless. I had never known family or deep connection outside of my mother, but it had always been the one thing I wished for—family, a sense of belonging, a place to call my own.

Tears streamed down my face. My heartbeat quickened, a warm feeling rising in my chest, overwhelming me with emotion. I couldn't hold it in any longer.

"Thank you, Miss Anna, for everything you did for me and Mama. I'm so sorry I never got to know you, but I know I would have loved you, just like Mama did."

The silence around me seemed to embrace me. I felt warmth—an undeniable presence—as if Miss Anna was wrapping me in a spirit-filled hug. Was this the healing Pastor Johnson said I needed?

But then I thought of Mama—how she loved me, yet kept so many secrets from me. Did she think I was too young or too weak to understand? Maybe she wanted to keep her past and her real life to herself. She always warned me about people, telling me they couldn't be trusted. But now, I was beginning to see that maybe she was warning me about herself.

As I walked home through the forest, I noticed I had company. An all-black Chevy Tahoe with Virginia license plates was parked along the dirt road, and what looked like Charlotte's mom's car was sitting in my driveway.

Mrs. Goodman stood on my front porch, along with a woman who looked like she could be a secret agent, both ringing the doorbell. The agent turned and noticed me walking up the dirt road behind them.

"Well, hello, you must be Ebony," the woman said, smiling like she already knew me. Her smile was warm, welcoming, and she smelled nice too.

"Hi, I'm Cheryl. Nice to meet you," she said, her voice smooth and confident.

"Hello, Cheryl. Hey, Miss Goodman," I greeted cautiously. "I didn't know you were coming by. I haven't spoken to Charlotte since the memorial. I've been taking things kinda slow," I admitted, feeling a twinge of sadness.

"I just got back from praying with the pastor at the church," I added, wondering why they were here unannounced.

"Ebony, that's good to hear. I've been concerned about you, living in this old house by yourself. How have you been doing?" Miss Goodman asked.

"I've been okay, honestly. Just taking it one day at a time," I replied.

"Yes, of course. This is Cheryl Woods. She's a private investigator working on your mother's case. We'd like to speak with you privately about it. Can we come in?"

"Oh… yes, ma'am. Of course. Please, come in."

"Thank you," they both replied as they stepped inside.

"Ebony, I know this is hard for you, and I can only imagine the pain you've endured these last few days, but we're here to ask you some questions and update you on your mother's case."

"So… did you find out what happened to her?" I asked, my eyes locked onto Miss Goodman.

"Well, as the mayor, I've been working closely with law enforcement here in McDillion, but the sheriff has decided to close the investigation into your mother's case. They claim they don't have the resources to get the answers we need. But that's why P.I. Woods is here. She's going to focus solely on this case. With the support of the McDillion Police Department and my office, we can find the killer and put them behind bars where they belong."

"So, my mother *was* killed?" My breath hitched.

"They told me it was some kind of freak accident. Miss Goodman, who would want to kill my mother?"

The questions poured out of me like a broken faucet. My heart pounded; my mind raced. What kind of nightmare was this? Why would the police lie to me? Why tell me something completely false that night at the station?

Cheryl Woods spoke up in a calm tone, clearly trying to ease my panic. "We have some new developments to share with you, but I'll need to ask you a few questions first."

"Okay, I guess... but then you'll answer *my* questions, right?"

"Of course we will, Ebony. We're here to help you. I know this is hard, but you're not alone," the mayor reassured me.

I took a deep breath, forcing myself to calm down. I had to focus. Cheryl leaned forward in the cushioned chair across from mine, placing her black leather bag on the floor. She pulled out a few folders, the kind that looked like they came straight from a school file cabinet.

"At what time of the day did you last speak with your mother before the incident?" she asked.

"Well, I saw Mama that morning. She made my favorite breakfast—shrimp and grits—to celebrate my graduation. We sat at the kitchen table, and I talked her head off about how much I loved the dress she bought me for the ceremony."

"Did she seem different to you in any way?"

"Take your time and think carefully, Ebony," Mayor Goodman added.

I closed my eyes, remembering that morning. Mama was wearing her favorite colored scrubs, dancing to her favorite tunes while eating breakfast. She was happy—so happy. Then there was a knock on the door.

The sudden ring of the mayor's cell phone snapped me back to reality. It startled me. "Excuse me, sorry for the interruption, but I need to take this call. I'll just be outside on the porch. Ebony, please continue with Miss Woods. You can trust her. Remember, she's here to help."

She stepped onto the porch, answering her call.
I turned back to Cheryl.

"Well… Mama *was* happy that morning. She'd been talking about my birthday for days, saying she had something special planned. But I don't know what that was."

I paused, sorting through the fragments of memory that grief had buried. "But on Saturday, I do remember there was a knock on the door."

Cheryl's pen hovered over her notepad. "Do you remember who it was? Or did you hear her speaking to someone?"

"No… I was walking back upstairs when she answered it. That's all I remember because my phone rang at the same time. Charlotte and I were excited about graduation, talking about our outfits."

"How was your mother's mood afterward?"

"Well, when I came back downstairs, she seemed quiet. But that wasn't unusual. One minute she'd be talking about work, then the next, she'd be silent—sometimes even sad."

Cheryl narrowed her eyes. "What do you mean by sad?"

I hesitated, then sighed. "Sometimes, Mama would stare out the window at night with the lights off, like she was looking for someone… or something. She always told me to watch my back, to never trust people because you never really know who they are."

Cheryl nodded slowly, intrigued. "Really?"

"Yes… and now I think she was right."

"Yeah, just like how I noticed your out-of-state license plate. She would always point them out, saying, 'Ebony, looks like those people are from Texas or Florida.' She taught me how to watch my back and always pay attention to my surroundings. But I just don't understand why she chose not to tell me the truth about other things," I said, my voice tinged with frustration. "I'm not a little girl anymore, you know. And I'm not weak. I *could* have handled the truth—*her* truth. It hurts to know that she didn't really trust me."

My eyes swelled with tears, the weight of disappointment pressing down on me. Embarrassed, I wiped them away quickly, trying to steady myself.

"Look, Ebony, I understand that you've been through some very traumatic shit lately," Miss Woods said, locking eyes with me, her voice firm yet understanding. She glanced toward the window, checking if the mayor was still on her call before turning back to me. "But you need to understand something—these things aren't just *happening* to you. They're preparing you."

"Preparing me?" I echoed, my voice barely above a whisper.

"Yes," she said without hesitation, her expression growing more serious.

"Preparing me for *what?*" I snapped, frustration bubbling to the surface.

"For the truth. The *whole* truth. And the ugly, painful, *hurtful* truth," she emphasized. "That's what. Now, are you ready for this truth? Do you think you can truly handle it?"

"Ebony," Miss Woods called my name again, but I didn't answer. I was too caught up in my own thoughts, bracing myself for something that I *knew*—deep down—was going to change me forever. Then, it happened.

A flash of light streaked across my vision, blinding me for a moment. For a split second, I saw nothing but brightness, and then, emerging from the void, stood a dark female figure. The same dark spirit from my nightmare the night before. It stood directly in front of me, its presence suffocating. Everything around me stilled. Miss Woods was frozen in place, her lips slightly parted, her eyes locked on mine, yet she didn't move.

"What's happening? What happened to her?" I tried to speak, but my voice felt distant, like it wasn't even coming from me.

"There is no fear. Don't be weak."

"Who are you?" I asked, my voice trembling.

"It's in your blood."

"I—I don't know who you are or what you're talking about."

"It is time. You are ready. Prepare yourself for this journey of truth. Listen to your inner wisdom. *The power is in your blood.*"

And just like that, the vision faded.

Reality came crashing back. The pounding of my heart roared in my ears, like the deep bass of a marching band drum. My breath hitched as dizziness crept over me, my lungs gasping for air.

Everything from the past few days rushed to the forefront of my mind. Just yesterday, I found a sacred journal book and a mystical black stone cross that I felt increasingly connected to. I discovered that I had some kind of ancestral power coursing through my veins. I received a brochure—out of nowhere—about my mother's university, one I never even knew she attended. I learned that I was a homeowner as of this Saturday, my eighteenth birthday.

And now, I was learning that my mother was murdered—and she had been hiding *massive* secrets from me my entire life.

"Ebony Blake, are you okay? Let me get you some water or something," Miss Woods' voice broke through my haze.

She reached for the glass I had left on the table earlier, her concern evident.

I blinked hard, shaking my head. "*Look,* I apologize if I came on too strong," she said, softening her tone. "I understand what it's like to lose a parent at an early age. I lost my father just a couple of years older than you, and I'm still not over it."

"Was he… killed too?" I asked, trying to steady my breath as I took a sip of my now-warm water.

"Yes, he was, actually." She exhaled deeply, her expression unreadable. "And I made a promise to myself that I would *do* something about it. That's the real reason I became a law enforcer—and later, a private investigator. I prefer to work on my own, help the community when I can, but on *my* terms."

Something about her confession made me feel like I could trust her.

And after what I had just experienced—what that *dark presence* had just shown me—I *knew* I needed to listen to her.

Miss Woods sat back down in her chair, taking a moment to collect herself as well. The room was thick with unspoken tension, an unshakable feeling that we were both teetering on the edge of something *big*.

I met her gaze, unwavering, and said, "*Okay,* Miss Woods. I'm ready. I *can* handle the truth. Please… tell me everything."

CHAPTER EIGHT

FAMILY

CHAPTER EIGHT
Family

Cassandra couldn't sleep at all that night. All she could think about was the conversation she had with the mayor of McDillion, Georgia. Lying flat on her back in her childhood bedroom, she stared at the ceiling. She had never even heard of McDillion, Georgia before today. She had been to Atlanta a few times and Savannah for various college administrator conferences, but McDillion had never crossed her radar. Her mind was racing, thoughts running a thousand miles a minute. How did this mayor get her phone number? Did she Google her, or did someone from the university pass along her information? And why did she think Cassandra's family had anything to do with this horrifying case? They had never been in the news or local papers for any scandal or bad reputation.

Well, she had just gone through a really bad divorce, but everyone experiences that at some point, especially at her age. Plus, how could she have known that her trifling husband at the time would cheat on her with a college student? That was embarrassing enough for her and her family. But this murder case? This just couldn't be happening.

After finally dozing off for about four hours, she awoke wide-eyed at five o'clock in the morning. She knew that was it for the night—her busy mind wouldn't allow her to sleep any longer. She took a shower and got dressed for the day, mentally mapping out everything she needed to accomplish after going to the office. First, she would research the university archives for any tragic events that occurred during that time period. Second, she would read up on McDillion, Georgia, and its mayor. Lastly, before leaving early for the upcoming weekend celebrations, she would have her assistant, Shannon, find whatever she could on Elaine Blake and email her the information. That way, she could take her time reviewing everything. Something about all of this felt off. She didn't fully understand why, but an unsettling feeling was creeping in, putting her in a mood she couldn't shake.

Being the oldest daughter of a high-profile family was a burden Cassandra carried with pride. It came with its own set of advantages and disadvantages, but after losing her own sister, she had learned early on that nothing was more important than family. Robert Junior, her younger brother, was overseas serving as a Marine, upholding a proud Bridges family tradition that dated back to their great-grandfather's service in the mid-to-late eighteenth century. With her brother away, she felt it was her duty to protect their family and its legacy. She needed to get to the bottom of this—fast.

After arriving at her office and checking off everything on her to-do list, Shannon messaged her, confirming that she had sent all the requested information to her email. Cassandra learned a great deal about McDillion and its historically preserved plantation lands, which had been passed down to its white descendants. She saw images of the McDillion Baptist Church and Miss Dee's Diner. There was also a striking picture of Mayor Gloria Goodman and her family, accompanied by articles detailing her recent election victory and her advocacy for women's rights. Cassandra liked what she saw and developed a newfound respect for Mayor Goodman.

She then asked Shannon, who had some downtime, to research the university archives for any past events and to gather information on Elaine Blake. But nothing could have prepared Cassandra for what she saw next.

A soul-piercing scream echoed through the top offices of the administration building, halting everyone in their tracks and stealing the breath of all who heard it. In the hallways, people rushed toward the source, guided by their ears, desperate to see what had happened. All eyes locked on Cassandra Bridges as she sat frozen at her desk, staring at her computer screen. Her wide eyes held an expression of utter shock and disbelief.

She had clicked on Shannon's email, which began with a live-breaking local news report on the Elaine Blake case. But the woman in the accompanying photo wasn't Elaine Blake. It was a picture of a dead woman. A middle-aged woman in her early forties—someone who was supposed to be long gone. But Cassandra recognized that face instantly. It was an adult photo of her little sister, Evelyn Bridges. And now she knew Evelyn had left behind a daughter.

Shannon's investigative skills were unmatched. As Cassandra scrolled further, she came across an image of a beautiful, brown-skinned girl, a perfect blend of Evelyn and someone else she couldn't quite place at the moment. But she knew the connection would come to her eventually.

"Miss Bridges, are you okay? Everyone heard you scream all the way down the hall."

"Oh my God, Shannon, please get the mayor of McDillion on the phone. I need to speak with her immediately," Cassandra shouted, tears welling in her eyes. "And get everyone out of here! They don't need to be looking into my office windows—I'm fine."

Shannon quickly ushered the curious crowd away, sending them back to their offices and classrooms. A few employees and students lingered, whispering amongst themselves, but Shannon made sure they all left. Moments later, Shannon's voice came through the speaker on Cassandra's office phone.

"Miss Bridges, I have the mayor on the line for you." Cassandra took a deep breath, steadying herself before pressing the button.

"Hello, Mayor Goodman. Can we talk? It's urgent."

The Divine Daughters

Cheryl quietly reached into her black leather tote, filled with various folders and documents, and placed a file labeled *Evelyn Bridges* on the coffee table between us. She looked directly at me and said, "Open it."

I glanced down at the folder, curiosity buzzing in my mind. Who was Evelyn Bridges? What did she have to do with my mother? My hands hesitated for only a second before I did as I was told and opened it.

"Mama?" The word left my lips in a breathless whisper. My eyes locked onto a photograph of a young female student at Old Town University. She had my mother's face—only twenty years younger. She had my mother's thick, curly, reddish-brown hair, her deep-set, shadowy eyes, and even that bright, unforgettable smile.

Everything about her was my mother—except her name. Her name was *Evelyn Bridges*. According to the file, she was born to Robert Bridges II and Violet Bridges. She had two siblings—Cassandra, her older sister, and Robert III, her younger brother. At Laketown University, she had been pursuing a Bachelor of Science in Nursing and was a member of the oldest and most elite sorority, *The Divine Daughters*.

I flipped through the folder, scanning photos of Evelyn at different events. My breath hitched when I came across one of Miss Woods, Evelyn, and several other young women, all smiling in front of the campus sign.

I looked up sharply. "Is that you, Miss Woods? You knew her?" My voice was edged with suspicion. "Is that why you were so nice to me earlier?"

Miss Woods met my gaze evenly. "Yes, I knew Evelyn very well. We grew up together. And I chose not to reveal that out of respect for you—and because there were things she didn't want you to know." She leaned forward, her expression gentle. "Honestly, I didn't want to scare you, Ebony."

Her voice softened even more. "I'm here to help you solve this case and find out what happened to my friend."

"Miss Woods, can I ask you a question?"

"Please, ask me anything."

"Are you a member of *The Divine Daughters*?"

"No," she admitted. "I was recruited at the same time as Evelyn, but unlike her, I wasn't chosen that year."

I hesitated for only a moment before standing abruptly. "Give me one second, Miss Woods. I have to show you something."

I ran upstairs to my mother's room, my heart pounding. I grabbed the mysterious book I had found among her things, cradling its heavy leather cover in both hands. As I turned to leave, I froze.

Miss Woods stood quietly in the doorway.

Uninvited, she stepped into the room, her eyes immediately landing on the book in my hands. A flicker of something—fear?—flashed across her face as she turned back to me.

"Ebony, don't show this to the mayor. Or to anyone else in this town." Her voice was firm. "No one can know you possess *The Divine Daughters'* sacred book."

I swallowed hard. "Can you help me understand it? I can read it, but I have so many questions."

Her brows furrowed. "Wait—you can *read* it? You can *see* the words?"

I nodded. She stared at me, stunned. "Only the chosen daughters can read the sacred book." Her voice dropped to a whisper. "Where did you get this? As far as I know, there are only three handwritten copies."

"I found it in my mother's things after she died," I said. "It was addressed to me. And check this out—the brochure for Laketown University was on my porch this morning, just sitting there by the door. That *has* to be a sign, right?"

Miss Woods exhaled sharply. "Evelyn must have left it for you. She must have wanted you to follow in her footsteps." Then, as if realizing something dark, her expression turned grave. "But wait—that could also mean *they* are looking for it."

Her eyes flickered to the book again. "This book has been missing from the university for years. It's a journal—every chosen daughter recorded her journey in it. It also…" Her voice trailed off, her lips pressing into a thin line.

"It *also* what?" I pressed.

She hesitated. "The book holds the records of every daughter who was chosen for *the sacrifice.*"

A chill slid down my spine.

Miss Woods grabbed my hand. "Look, just promise me you won't show this to anyone else. Keep it safe."

I met her gaze. "Okay. I promise."

She exhaled in relief. "Good. Now, let's get back downstairs before the mayor returns."

As we walked down the stairs, I glanced at her. "You scared me, you know? Sneaking up behind me like that."

She gave me a small smile. "I didn't mean to scare you. But I'm a private investigator, Ebony. My intuition is my gift. I move when my spirit tells me to. And it told me to follow you—to protect whatever secret you were carrying."

I raised an eyebrow. "Interesting. So, we all have secret spiritual gifts?"

Miss Woods shook her head. "No, not everyone. But the children of the old Laketown community *definitely* do. It's in our blood. It's what sets us apart. A gift from our ancestors."

I felt my stomach drop. That was exactly what the *darkness* had said in my dream last night. We sat back down in the living room. "Miss Woods," I asked cautiously, "why did my mother change her name and identity?"

Before she could answer, the front door creaked open. Mayor Goodman stepped inside, her face clouded with concern, her eyes sharp—like she *knew* something we didn't. She glanced at the file on the coffee table, then back at me.

"Ebony, are you okay? I can't imagine how you're taking all of this. So many secrets, so much truth—revealed in such a short period of time. It would make any adult lose their mind."

I took a steadying breath. "It *is* a lot. But I'm ready for the truth. My spirit feels at peace, like this is what I *need* to know. My mind has been racing for years with unanswered questions, and now I'm ready for answers, Mayor Goodman."

I hesitated. "I want to heal. But it's hard when you don't have a family." The words ached coming out.

"All I ever wanted was a loving family," I admitted. "But I understand that's not in the cards for everyone. Some people just have a mother or father who cares for them, and that's it. I'll be eighteen this Saturday, and this will be the first time I spend it alone."

Mayor Goodman's expression softened. "I know you feel that way, but Charlotte would *never* allow that to happen. She doesn't leave for Atlanta until next week."

I smiled at the mention of her daughter. "I'm so excited for her. She's been dreaming of going to Spelman forever. She's going to be a lawyer, just like you. You must be so proud."

"I am," she said, a tinge of sadness in her voice. "But I'm going to miss her."

Then she straightened. "But let's get back on track with this case. What did I miss?"

Miss Woods briefed her, carefully leaving out any mention of the book. Mayor Goodman turned back to me. "Ebony, I don't know why your mother changed her name and left her home. But I wanted to tell you directly—my family cares for you. We'll always be here for you. But as mayor, I have many hats to wear, and this will be my last visit. As you move forward, take care of yourself. Be open to the change that's coming."

I swallowed. "I *hope* it's a good change, Mayor Goodman. Because I've had enough bad ones lately."

She smiled sadly. "Stay prayed up, honey. God never gives us more than we can handle. Trust me, we've all seen hard times, but we're still standing."

Then she left. As I watched her drive away, I turned to Miss Woods.

"Well," I muttered, "that was *interesting*."

Miss Woods nodded. "Please call me Cheryl. Whoever she was talking to on that call... *changed her mind about this case entirely*."

The Call

"Hello, Cassy. Yes, of course—Is everything okay?"

Mayor Goodman was startled by the sound of heavy breathing on the other end of the line. She waited curiously, her patience steady, sensing the urgency in Cassandra's silence.

"Mayor Goodman, after looking over Old Town University's archives and conducting my own research into this case, I have found some very disturbing information. But first, I need to know—how exactly did you connect this case to me and my family?"

"Well, Miss Bridges, as I mentioned on our previous call, after the McDillion police concluded their investigation, we began searching for the child's next of kin. The medical examiner, using dental records, traced her DNA back to your prominent family line. That's how we confirmed that Elaine Blake was somehow related to you."

Cassandra's tone sharpened. "Who gave you my family's phone number? Did you Google us?"

She wasn't just asking—she was interrogating. She needed to understand how this woman had linked her family to a murder. Did she know Evelyn's secret all along? Was she working with someone to bring harm to the Bridges name?

"Look, Miss Bridges," the mayor replied, her voice firm but calm, "I understand that this case is unsettling. But I have no hidden agenda—I'm simply trying to find a family for Ebony. She's alone and confused right now. Can you even imagine what that child is going through? She just graduated from high school, and now, after her mother's tragic murder, she has no one."

Cassandra exhaled sharply. "I know you're her mayor, but why are *you* so invested in this case?"

There was a brief pause before Mayor Goodman responded. "Because my daughter cares. Ebony and my daughter, Charlotte, have been best friends for over ten years. This case has deeply affected my family. We were the ones who helped lay Elaine Blake's ashes to rest. We want to make sure that Ebony is taken care of."

Cassandra sighed, her grip tightening around the phone. "Okay, I understand now. Please accept my apologies. Just an hour ago, I found out that my little sister—who I thought had been *dead* for over twenty years—was alive all this time. Not only that, but she had a daughter. A daughter named Ebony." She swallowed hard, steadying her emotions. "And by the way, I'll be in McDillion tomorrow to collect my niece *before* someone kills her like they did her mother."

"I'm so sorry for your loss, Miss Bridges," Mayor Goodman said softly. "I'll let Ebony know to expect company tomorrow."

"Oh, and one more thing," Cassandra added, her voice now cold and resolute. "You and your administration should be expecting a call from our lawyers very soon. Because this is *not* over, Mayor Goodman. You haven't even begun to feel the power and influence of the founding family of Laketown, Virginia."

There was no goodbye. Just the sharp *click* of the call ending.

Cassandra sat in silence for a moment, gripping the phone in her lap, her body tense with anger, grief, and disbelief. The emotions hit her like waves crashing against the shore.

How had her sister lived all these years without her? How had she kept such a massive secret—an entire child—without the family knowing?

How could she turn her back on *everything*—their traditions, their name, their legacy?

Cassandra drove home in a daze, the rain beginning to pour as she navigated the dark roads in her black Land Rover Defender. Tears blurred her vision, but she didn't stop them. She let them fall freely, grief and rage tangled in the storm.

For twenty years, she had mourned a sister who was never dead. And now, she had a niece she had never known. And someone—someone out there—wanted that girl gone.

THE DEAD BODY

CHAPTER NINE
The Dead Body

Ebony

"So now that the mayor is gone, can you *please* tell me what is going on with the sacred journal? And why do we have to keep it such a secret?" I asked Cheryl.

She leaned forward slightly, lowering her voice. "Look, it's like this—*everybody ain't your friend*, and you really need to watch your back."

I scoffed. "Now you sound like my mother. She used to say that to me *all the time*—anytime I tried to make a new friend or even tried out for something at school, that's exactly what she'd say."

The moment felt heavy, and I needed to shift the mood. "Tell me, Cheryl... how long were you and my mama friends?"

Cheryl's expression softened. "Well, your mother and I grew up together in Laketown, Virginia—*Old* Laketown, to be exact. We were friends all through high school and even went to college together. She was *brilliant*—top of the class, even. And back then, she was *very* involved in the church."

Listening to her talk about my mother was like hearing about a *stranger*. She spoke of my mama playing sports, running track, and even how they had once dreamed about joining the same sorority together.

It all felt... surreal. But one question sat on my tongue, heavy and unspoken. When I finally asked it, Cheryl's whole demeanor changed.

"So, tell me... *what is the mayor hiding from me?*" I paused, watching her carefully. "And Cheryl—how *did* my mother die?"

She exhaled, then slowly bent down, reaching into her bag. She pulled out a file labeled *Elaine Blake* and laid it on the coffee table. Without a word, she flipped it open and placed a single photograph in front of me.

"To be brutally honest with you, Ebony," she began, her voice grave, "your mother's body was *mutilated*. Her throat and both wrists were *slit* with an extremely sharp object. Blood was drained and *collected* from her body."

A sharp, guttural scream tore from my chest before I even realized I was making a sound. It was the loudest noise I had *ever* created. My breath felt ripped from my lungs, leaving me dizzy, my body swaying, completely overwhelmed.

"Oh my God… Cheryl, *who* would do something like this to her? *How* is it that the police have *no leads* on her killer?" My hands trembled as I dropped the gruesome photograph onto the floor.

Cheryl's voice was steady. "The killer was waiting for her outside, near her car in the parking lot. But she had parked in a blind spot—no cameras could capture the attack. The only footage they have is a dark figure moving toward her, then vanishing into the trees that surround the lot."

I shook my head in disbelief. "No *trace*? No fingerprints? No hair? Nothing?"

Cheryl nodded. "Nothing."

My mind reeled. "I *have* to find out who did this to my mother. I know she wasn't the *best* mom in the world, but she didn't deserve to *die* like this." My voice cracked. "This feels *personal* to me for some reason."

I swallowed hard, trying to steady myself. "My mama drove an old Chevy Impala, so breaking into it wouldn't have been difficult. But *why* kill her? And *why* take her blood?"

A chill ran through me as a phrase I had heard *too many times* echoed in my mind. *It's in our blood.* Something inside me told me the answers were hidden in the sacred journal. Without another word, I reached for *The Divine Daughters'* book and began reading from the very beginning. I needed to know *who* these women were. *What* made them so special? And most importantly—what was in *our blood* that made someone kill my mother *for it?*

Cheryl

Oh, God… I felt *horrible*. Why hadn't Evelyn *prepared* Ebony for this? If she had the missing *Divine Daughters* journal, she *had* to have known that dark forces would come for her one day. If Ebony had grown up with the truth, if she had been raised by her *real* family—the *Bridges*—she wouldn't be this *weak*.

Evelyn… what *have* you done?

Looking at Ebony was like staring at a *more beautiful* version of her mother. My heart ached for her. I was still in shock over Evelyn's murder. But as I sat there, I started thinking—*who in the hell* would kill a woman, drain her blood, and *collect* it?

Why *just* the blood?

Whoever did this… *had been watching her.*

I had a feeling they *also* knew about Ebony.

A slow smile crept across my face as I thought of the one person who might have answers.

My *mother*. A *Woods Woman*.

For centuries, the Woods Women—healers who lived in the pine forests—had been sought after for their wisdom. They had gifts *straight from the earth*. They were the original creators of medicine and had survived *every* imaginable hardship. I hadn't spoken to my mother in a couple of days. It was time to give her a call.

"Ebony, I know someone who can help us," I said, standing. "I'm gonna make a call."

Ebony nodded, her eyes glued to the journal. "Okay, I'll be here reading."

I stepped outside and dialed.

"Hello?"

"Hey, Ma. How are you?"

"Oh, hey, honey! How's everything going?"

I sighed. "Well, I *meant* to call earlier, but I've been tied up with a new case."

"Let me guess," she chuckled, "it's that murder in Georgia, huh?"

I smiled. "You *always* know when I'm onto something."

"Of course I do. You *lit up* when you saw it on the news. So tell me—how's it going?"

"Actually... *really* well. I've been given full access to the case files in both McDillion and Virginia."

"Well, that's wonderful, Cheryl! But remember what I always tell you—*be the best listener and follow your intuitive spirit.*"

"I do, Ma," I assured her. "Always. But I was actually calling because I need your insight. I have a weird question."

"Go on, then."

"Who do you think would *murder* someone and *drain their blood?*"

There was silence on the line. Then—

"They *took her blood?*" My mother's voice dropped to a whisper. "Oh, my God..."

I gripped the phone. "Do you know something, Ma?"

She hesitated. "It's been a long time since these things happened to women. *Years ago*, certain *rituals* required women to lose their *hearts*, but not their *blood*. But if you're dealing with a *blood collector... they wanted her power.*"

I froze.

"Who, Ma? *Who* would want her power?"

Her voice turned solemn.

"When I was young, I once went with my mother on her herb deliveries. We stopped at *The Temple of God's Anointed*—McDillion's church. I wandered down the wrong hallway and... I saw something."

I swallowed. "What did you see?"

She exhaled. "Bishop Washington *Senior* was leading a *ceremony*. He slit open a *human heart*, drank the blood, and passed it to his *son*—as a *blessing*."

My blood ran cold.

"I *knew* there was something wrong with that church," I whispered.

"That's why I *always* warned you about them," she said. "Cheryl... *you have no idea* how powerful the Holy Bishop is."

And suddenly, I *knew*.

This case was *bigger* than I ever imagined.

And Ebony?

She was *right in the middle of it.*

"Honey, I told your father, and he didn't believe me. He would always say that I was just being crazy. He didn't want me to spread my foolishness to you and get it in your head. He was the one who was excited about you pledging for the Divine Daughters."

"Yeah, I remember you trying to talk me out of it. You never liked the idea of me being that close to the church, I said in response."

"Yep, and now you know why, Mama said, taking a deep breath and calming down. So, do you think a blood-collecting murderer possibly has something to do with the Temple of God's Anointed?"

Before my mother could respond, my phone started to beep, showing that the mayor was calling in on the other line. I needed to answer it to see what was going on with her. She seemed very distant and a little overwhelmed before she left earlier.

"Oh Ma, let me call you back. I have another call coming in. Thank you so much for your help and for sharing that story with me. I'm gonna do some more research on the Holy Bishop to back up this case. I'll talk to you later. Love you."

"Okay, Cheryl, you're welcome, honey. Love you too."

"Hello, Mayor Goodman. How are you doing?" I asked to get a feel for her mental state.

"Hello, Cheryl. How did everything go with Ebony? How is she after hearing the truth about her mother's death?"

"Well, to be honest, she did better than I expected after seeing her mother's file and photos of her body."

"What? Oh my goodness, you showed her that too? I guess anyone would have had a horrific reaction, right?"

"Well, I guess so, but I felt horrible about it. She has to know the truth if we are going to move forward with this case, I said, trying to calm down the guilt in my mind."

"Yes, that is why I'm calling you." When we first spoke on the phone, I told you that my main goal was to keep my promise to my daughter to find Ebony's family so that she wouldn't be alone dealing with all of this craziness. Because of you, Private Investigator Woods, we know who her family is, and soon she will too. I have spoken to her Aunt Cassandra

Bridges, and she will be here tomorrow to meet Ebony and take her back to their estate in Virginia.

"Oh wow, that's good news for her. I'm sure that Ebony will be excited about that. But what about her mother's murder case? Are we still working on it?"

"Actually, the Bridges are now involving their lawyers and plan to sue me and the city of McDillion if Elaine Blake is proven to be their long-lost relative. So, to answer your question—no. As of right now, this case is closed and awaiting legal action."

"Wow, that's crazy. I'm sorry for all of the trouble this has caused you and your family. But at least Ebony and her family will find closure. At some point, this will all be over soon."

"Cheryl, please inform Ebony of the news and have her pack her bags for Old Laketown, Virginia. Cassandra Bridges will be arriving before noon tomorrow."

Driving home from Ebony's house, Mayor Goodman's cell phone rang. She answered it, thinking it might be her husband or Charlotte calling, and praying that it wasn't Cassandra Bridges calling her back.

"Mayor Goodman speaking", she answered in her professional tone, just in case.

"Yes, hello, Mayor Goodman, this is Detective Myra James from McDillion police. I'm calling because I was told that you have a detective on the Blake case."

"Yes, I did, but as of today, I was told that it was closed due to lack of resources and manpower. Who is this? I'm sorry—you said your name was Myra James?"

"Yes, Mayor Goodman. I am new to the McDillion team, transferring from out of state, but that's not why I've called you this evening."

"Oh, okay. Well, how can I help you, Miss James?"

"Can you please have your private investigator meet me at the corner of Hospital Boulevard and Westley Lane? Another dead body has been found in the woods."

"What! I'll call her right away. Be looking for Cheryl Woods to meet you there, the mayor said with authority in her voice, but inside, she felt shocked and unprepared for this."

Gloria Goodman pulled into the next gas station to calm herself and make the call to Cheryl. Sitting in her white Mercedes, she started to think about her town and what was happening. She sat up in her soft peanut butter-colored leather seat and took a deep breath.

"Hello, Cheryl, we have a problem. The McDillion police are keeping the Blake case open. They have found a second dead body in the woods."

"Oh my god, that's crazy. Where is it, and how can I help?" Cheryl asked.

"They have a new detective who has been transferred in. Her name is Myra James. She is who you will be working with. I need you to meet her right away at the corner of Hospital Boulevard and Westley Lane. Please keep me updated with the progress of this case."

"I'm on it, Mayor Goodman."

The Dead Doctor

At the end of the road that leads to the McDillion hospital, at its last cross street, Wesley Lane, sat an all-black Cadillac Escalade empty on the side of the road. Wesley Lane is the long road that leads to the gated community on the other side of the train tracks. However, along the two-lane road are trees and thick wooded landscapes. The long pine trees have large trunks that are easily hundreds of years old. There are deer signs to keep the residents aware and to drive safely through the wooded areas.

When Cheryl pulled up, the scene was easy to find because the police and ambulance were there. The traffic was backed up for a while, too, but the officers were directing people in a slow and steady manner. People were driving slowly as they passed the scene, wondering what happened in their small, boring town. Some stopped to ask the officers what had happened but received no response while being asked to proceed forward cautiously.

As Cheryl parked and walked toward the scene, she showed her badge to the officers, who then called for Detective James, who was speaking with the eyewitness at the time.

"Hey, you must be Cheryl Woods, the private investigator on the Blake case?"

"Yes, and you are Myra James, correct?"

"I just transferred from up north but got right to work as soon as I arrived."

"So, tell me, Detective James, what do we have here? Cheryl asked."

"Well, we have a forty-seven-year-old man, named Lloyd Gaines, who, based on his identification, was a doctor at the hospital. His body was found in the woods about a ten-minute walk from his vehicle, the detective explained."

"Are you up to date on the Blake case?" Cheryl asked.

"Yes, I reviewed the file, and I noticed some similarities."

"Like what?" Cheryl asked.

"Well, the victim's body was dragged into the woods, and his neck was sliced as well. But he bled out at the scene, and there were no sliced wrists," Myra replied.

"Okay, so it seems that this could be the same killer, but maybe he had a different motive for this murder," Cheryl said.

"Maybe. I also spoke with the eyewitness who found the body in the woods. The old man is very shaken up by the whole thing because he's never seen a dead body before in real life. He's over there by the ambulance if you want to speak with him," Myra pointed out.

"Hello, I'm Private Investigator Cheryl Woods, working this case with Detective James. You spoke with her earlier, correct?"

"Oh yes," the old man responded, as if she had interrupted his deep thoughts.

"Your name?" Cheryl asked, pulling out her notepad to collect his statement.

"Jon Rogers."

"So, tell me, Mister Rogers, about what time did you find the body here in the woods?"

"Maybe about an hour or so ago."

"How often do you come out here?"

"I've been walking Ralphy out this way for about five years now. He loves it out here 'cause he can always find something to chase."

"Really? How far away do you live from the scene?"

"I'm about a mile or so up the road."

"So, tell me again what happened."

"Well, just like I told the other lady, I was out here walking Ralphy like I do every day. Then he started going crazy, barking out of control. So, I let him go to see what he found. Hell, I thought he might have found a dead bird or something. But never did I ever think it would be a dead body."

"So, what did you do after that?"

"Well, after the shock of it all, I grabbed my cell phone and called nine-one-one. They got here about ten to fifteen minutes later."

"What did the body look like when you saw it?"

"I could see the head and one hand—the rest was covered in dirt, buried under leaves."

"Did you ever hear a car or truck at any time in the area while you were walking your dog?"

"No, it was real quiet out here. I don't remember hearing anything."

"Thank you so much for your statement, Mister Rogers."

"You're welcome. I'll make sure to say a prayer for his family."

"I'm sure they'll need it."

Myra was working with the officers at the scene, gathering information and collecting evidence. She seemed experienced and well-spoken, but feisty in her own way. She stood about five feet tall, brown-skinned with short black hair. She wore tight jeans, a light blue blouse, and black comfortable boots, with a black blazer left open as she moved around, taking charge of the investigation.

"Anything new from the witness?" Cheryl asked.

"No, not really, but he's a little shaken up about the whole thing. He might be rethinking how safe this trail really is."

"Well, I'm sure he can find another one in these dense forests."

"Woods, let me show you something. I was looking at the trees and branches close to where the body was found, and I think I spotted some tracks. What do you think?"

Cheryl knelt down to get a better look. With both hands, she touched the soil, and in her mind's eye, the footprints began to reveal themselves within the grass and leaves. Each step was highlighted in a light green glow. She smiled to herself, grateful for the favor Mother Earth had shown her. It had been months since she had spent time in her ancestral habitat, and now, when she needed help the most, the woods were guiding her to the killer.

"Yeah, I think you're right, James. These do look like tracks. Looks like they lead south, back towards the road. And they're definitely male—the size alone tells you that."

"Absolutely. I'll get some spray paint to mark them and see how far south they go."

While Myra went to grab the spray paint, Cheryl took a moment to give thanks. Reflecting on what had just happened, she looked forward to sharing the event with her mother later.

"A few of the guys are gonna stay and take photos, looking for any additional clues that might help us. But can you meet me at the station? I want to review the security tape from the Blake case with you."

"Sure. What about all this out here?"

"Don't worry, they'll bring the evidence to us, and we'll review the body with the examiner in a couple of hours."

"Okay, looks like it's gonna be a long night."

"Yep. Good thing we've got plenty of coffee."

Driving in her all-black Tahoe, Cheryl had the new murder case heavy on her mind. A dead Black man, throat slit, blood drained—yet barely any evidence left at the scene. How was he able to do this without making a mess? So many thoughts ran through her head.

Her phone rang.

"Hello."

"Hey, Ma."

"Cheryl, how's it going? Are you on your way back?"

"No. I thought I was gonna be when I spoke to you hours ago, but that all changed after that phone call."

"Really? What happened?"

"There's been another killing. And this time, it's a man."

"Does he have his throat slit like the last case?"

"Yep, and his body is drained of blood, too. This is just crazy. I don't get why this person is going around killing people and taking their blood."

"Well, you're definitely dealing with a blood collector for sure. I wonder what they're planning to do with it all."

"Ma, guess what? You're gonna love this."

"What? Tell me—you know I hate surprises."

"I was at the scene in the woods, and I placed my hands in the soil. My request was heard, and the forest showed me the way. It lit up the footsteps of the possible killer."

"What? You mean Mother Earth heard you and connected with you? That's amazing news! I'm so happy for you, Cheryl."

"Thanks, Ma."

"You know our planet mother is always there, waiting on you to desire her presence in your life."

"I know. But after Dad was killed, I just lost the desire for her. I felt like that part of me had died too. But tonight, I felt reborn in a way. I felt special. She really does love us, Ma."

"Absolutely. And I'm just happy that you are finally starting to realize that truth at your own pace, daughter. We are Woods Women—that's in your blood, and that will never change. We are special because of our ancestors' sacrifice. Be very proud of that."

"I am, Ma. And I'm thankful."

CHAPTER TEN
FAMILY

CHAPTER TEN
Family

Wet from the rain, Cassandra quietly entered her family home. Heartbroken from the day's events, she placed her bag down in the foyer and went straight to the wine cellar at the far end of the kitchen pantry. She grabbed an oldie but goodie to enjoy all by herself.

Mason, who always exuded his formal yet militant training, entered the kitchen silently but remained observant. He had been with the Bridges family since he was a young man and had watched Cassandra grow into the woman she was today. He could always tell when something was troubling the woman destined to be the next matriarch of the great Bridges family. His heart had felt for her over the years. Cassandra had endured so much. He remembered as if it were yesterday—the day her sister went missing and was later declared dead. He had been a pallbearer at the funeral for Mr. Robert Bridges. He had stood by Miss Violet, Cassandra's mother, when Cassandra lost her twins and divorced her abusive husband. He had been there to help Cassandra move back home permanently to be close to her mother.

Mason had always been there for this family; they were his family, and they had never treated him as anything less. As long as he respected his position and took his duties seriously, he would always have a place here. He truly loved this family more than anything or anyone else in the world.

"Miss Cassy, let me," he said politely, reaching for the bottle to open it and pouring it into a beautiful red wine glass.

"Mason, thank you so much. I don't know how you do it, but you are always there when we need you."

"It is my pleasure, Miss," Mason said with a smile.

"You would not believe the day I've had. I can barely put my thoughts together to comprehend it myself."

"It's okay, Miss. Just try to relax. I find that reflecting on one's day in a more relaxed state helps the mind process events better, leading to wiser decision-making."

"Mason, again, I totally understand why my father refused to separate himself from you. You are a vessel of wisdom. A true man of honor. I am so thankful for your presence in our lives." Cassandra's words created puddles of tears that slowly awaited their turn to fall from her eyes.

"It has always been my pleasure to serve this great house, Miss Cassy. But your words this evening have truly pierced my soul. My spirit has been heavy as of late. I feel that there is a change in the air. But thank you, Miss. If you need anything, please don't hesitate to call," Mason replied, holding back his emotions as he silently exited the kitchen to return to his quarters.

Cassandra turned back to her glass and bottle of her favorite Cabernet from Old Laketown's local winery. All she could think about was her baby sister and the possible hell she had endured in her hidden life. She knew she needed to speak to her mother about everything before bringing a teenage girl into their home. Yet, a part of her was starting to look forward to having a young person around. She had wanted so badly to have a daughter, but after losing her babies and her marriage, she had allowed that dream to die. She had never wanted to love again or even give it a chance. Cassandra had become so cold—it was her way of dealing with the tremendous loss in her life. But she knew that if Ebony was truly her niece, she would recognize it immediately. The women in her mother's bloodline were powerful. Even though they no longer practiced their ancestral methods and gifts, their spirits remained real and would reveal themselves to confirm the dormant power within. She had to go to her mother to prepare before she left in the morning.

Napping in her cozy chair in her Victorian-themed bedroom, which matched the beautiful Victorian-style home, Violet slept peacefully. But that peace soon shattered when another nightmare took hold.

In her dream, a girl was haunted by the fear of death or being consumed by darkness. She ran for her life, knowing the enemy was coming. Her bare feet pierced the cold, hard soil with every swift step forward. In her third trimester, she knew she shouldn't be running, but she would do anything to protect the new life growing inside her. Out of breath, she leaned against a tree, but the ache and pain were unbearable. A moan escaped her lips, the sound of agony and fear. She looked back for the enemy, but no one was there.

Sweat dripped from her brow, stinging her eyes and leaving a bitter taste on her lips. She gasped for breath, clutching her womb as sudden warmth spread between her thighs. Blood and water trickled down her legs, shocking her system. As she fell, bracing herself, blood covered her feet, its stench suffocating.

She had left a trail. It was only a matter of time before the enemy found her. Her heart ached for the child she carried, but she knew shame and fear would haunt her forever. She could not see her enemy, but she felt their presence. The darkness thickened, shrouding her vision. The ground trembled, and cracks formed behind her, filled with liquid fire.

"I'm coming for you, my love," a deep voice echoed in the air. "You can't run forever. I will find you. I need your blood."

Startled and afraid, Violet screamed. She awoke, panic-stricken, and called for Mason. The distinguished gentleman entered the master bedroom, his face filled with concern.

"Madam, are you okay? Did you have another nightmare?" he asked gently.

"Oh, Mason, I keep having the same bad dreams. It's like the spirit is trying to tell me something, but I can't understand. Something dark is in the air—I can feel it." Violet clutched her chest, her heart pounding.

"I'll make you some chamomile tea. It always helps to calm your nerves, Miss. I'll be right back. Just try to relax."

"Thank you so much, Mason."

Cassandra ran upstairs, passing Mason on his way down.

"Momma! Momma, are you okay? I thought I heard you scream."

"Oh, Cassy, I didn't know you were home so soon. Yes, I had another nightmare. It's been happening since last weekend. My spirit has been so heavy."

"Well, I think I know why," Cassandra said, her eyes glossy with emotion.

"What are you talking about?"

"Momma, I have some disturbing news to share, and I think you should sit down."

"Cassandra, you're scaring me. You know I'm too old for crazy shit. Tell me what's going on."

Cassandra inhaled deeply. "A couple of days ago, I received a phone call from the mayor of a small town called McDillion, Georgia. She informed me that a woman named Elaine Blake had been murdered in her town. After completing the autopsy, the medical examiner revealed that this woman was not Elaine Blake but Evelyn Bridges—your daughter— who was pronounced dead twenty years ago."

A sudden crash shattered the silence. Mason had returned with Violet's tea, but in his shock, he dropped the glass.

"I'm so sorry, Madam. I'll bring another after I clean this up." His voice trembled, his eyes full of shock, confusion, and terror.

"What? That can't be. My Evelyn was buried. That just can't be. Murdered? No… that cannot be."

"I had the same response, Mama, but then I had my assistant do some research on the case, and she sent me the information. Look at this," Cassandra said as she turned her cell phone toward her mother to view the screen.

The first thing that popped up was the news report and the recent picture of Elaine Blake. The scream that erupted from Violet's mature lungs caused Cassandra and Mason to fall to the floor, covering their ears with their hands.

"No, this can't be. This can't be."

The pictures on the wall began to fall, and the tall mirror on the wall cracked loudly.

"How could this be? He promised me, and he never breaks his promises. Dear God, how could this be?"

The atmosphere shifted, and the lights throughout the house flickered. Violet's tears were endless and soon turned to blood as her body began to shake uncontrollably.

Cassandra had never seen her mother in this state, but Mason had. He had been there twenty years ago when this tragedy first occurred. Mason braced himself along the door, quickly ran to Cassandra, and grabbed her hand.

"Miss, we have to go. We must leave her," he pleaded.

"No, Mason, I can't leave her like this. What is happening?"

"It's the Great Mother," Mason responded. "Please come with me. Let us return when the pain subsides."

"All these years I have served him faithfully, and this is how I'm treated. How dare they do this to my daughter, my own flesh and blood? This does not bring glory to our Lord. This just can't be!" Violet continued to shout and vent as she paced within the master bedroom.

The two left the room, shut the door, and collapsed in the hallway.

"Mason, what the hell was that? What just happened to my mother?" Cassandra asked, shocked.

"Miss Cassandra, let us go downstairs and speak privately in the kitchen, please," he responded in a calming manner.

After carefully walking downstairs and sitting at the table, Cassandra couldn't stop shaking. Her body continued to tremble with fear. Terrified of what her mother had become, she reached for her glass of Cabernet, and Mason began to pour.

"Miss Cassandra, do you know how I got here?" Mason asked. Cassandra looked up at him, suddenly realizing that she did not know how or when he had entered into service with her family.

"No, Mason, I don't believe I do. I just remember you always being here. I know that when I was little, you spent most of your time with Daddy working and helping with the town council. But please, tell me—how did you become the man you are now?"

"Well, Miss Cassandra, I am a direct descendant of the Royal Moors of the British Crown. My great-great-great-grandfather was a Black-a-Moor who helped establish the Freedmen's Estate here in America. They were spies sent forth to report back to the king's court. After the plantation hands revolted, many Black people came from far and wide to be part of such greatness. My father and many other Moors came and helped build the Old Laketown neighborhood. It was my grandfather who, through a protective covenant with your grandfather, helped establish powerful influence that aided in forming leadership and governance here in Laketown. We are credited for the Victorian-style construction and old stone roads. Because of their masterful work, many tourists still visit today to witness their exquisite designs."

"That's why my father held you in such high regard," Cassandra replied.

"Yes, but it was my father who introduced your father to your mother."

"Really? How?" Cassandra asked.

"Your mother comes from a long line of diviner women—dark power witches whose magic comes from the moon and earth, and most importantly, the dark angel Maryan. They are the originators of The Divine Daughters, a sorority of powerful women. They were chosen centuries ago by Maryan, princess of hell, to bring forth her power and influence on the earth."

"Wait, what? So you mean to tell me that my mother is a witch? Does that mean I am too?"

"Yes and no. Even though you carry her bloodline, only one daughter can receive the ancestral gift, and unfortunately, that daughter was Evelyn."

"When your mother lost Evelyn, she lost so much more—her ancestral heritage and the blessing she would have received from the Holy Bishop."

"But Mason, what does the Holy Bishop and our church have to do with this?" Cassandra asked, searching for clarity.

"Well, he is the one truly anointed by the god of this earth, Sheiton. The Divine Daughters serve him through the church."

Cassandra grabbed her glass, chugged the rest of her wine, and said, "What did you just say to me? Wait a minute—did you just say that the devil is the god of the earth? Mason, pour me another glass, please…"

"I know that based on your religious teachings, this sounds crazy and blasphemous, but this is the truth that the Great Roman Church conceals from the public. Only the royals and the most powerful are aware. But it is implied in Second Corinthians, chapter four, verse four, that Satan is the god of this world. Also, in First John, chapter five, verse nineteen, it states that the wicked one holds authority over all cultural systems on earth."

"It's amazing how the truth is hidden right in front of us, and people just don't see it or don't believe it," Cassandra said, contemplating the Bible's hidden messages.

"Miss Cassandra, now that you know the truth and have witnessed your mother in a chaotic state, I pray that you tread lightly. The shock of this grave news has caused her to relapse. For years after your sister's mysterious death, she vowed to put aside her ancestral practice and take on the ways of the church. The Holy Bishop and her devotion to the church became her substitute, denying her actual truth. But now, I fear that we don't know what state of mind she could be in," Mason said with reverential fear in his voice.

Cassandra had never seen Mason so scared, yet he still exuded confidence in who he was and the truth he knew.

"The crazy thing is, I didn't even get to tell her about Ebony."

Suddenly, Violet walked into the kitchen, her pupils ruby red, her skin smooth as silk, her face at least ten years younger. She no longer stood hunched, slow, and out of breath. Violet stood tall, renewed, her health restored, and her confidence undeniable. Her truth had set her free, and her energy matched it.

"Then tell me now, daughter—who is this Ebony that you speak of?"

Cassandra slowly placed her wine glass on the table, her eyes fixed on her mother. Terrified of her response but too scared to lie, she said to her mother, the dark divine witch, "Ebony is your granddaughter—Elaine Blake's, or rather, Evelyn's, only child."

"My Evelyn had a child? I have a granddaughter. I'm so shocked by all of this. She is a teenager and will eighteen this Saturday."

As Violet's spirit calmed, the red in her eyes faded to deep brown, and the paleness in her skin warmed to a golden hue with rosy cheeks.

"Cassandra, you must bring the child home."

"Yes, Mama. I leave for her early in the morning."

"What, oh my god, that means we have a birthday and an ancient ceremony to prepare for. I look forward to meeting my granddaughter. Her name is now… Ebony Bridges," Violet said with a purposeful mind.

Violet stood directly in front of her daughter, grabbed her face, and spoke softly.

"Cassandra, you have always been the strong one. I can always depend on you to do what is right and to protect this great house. You are a Bridges—never forget how powerful you are, my beloved child."

DAUGHTER

CHAPTER ELEVEN
Daughter

Ebony Meets Onyx

"Wake up."

The sound of my own voice caused my eyes to open. A dark version of me stood over me and spoke. She had eyes like rubies and locs that reached her waistline. She wore a black-stoned cross around her neck and exuded a fierce spirit.

"We don't have much time. The blood harvest moon is coming, and we must prepare," she said, then grabbed my hand to pull me up.

"But… are you me? Who are you? You look like me, but you're not me," I said in awe and confusion.

"I am Onyx, your dark spirit—the version of you that has been dormant within. I am the part of you your mother has tried to protect you from. But her lies and manipulation will never change our destiny. Lies are of Malphas, the prince of hell, and Christians who lie and live in their lies are actually his children. He has planted many within the church from the beginning."

"What do you mean?" I asked, because I could feel the truth in every word she said. The anger and pain from my mother lying to me every day of my life still burned deep within me.

"You know exactly what I mean. I can feel the fire lit deep within your belly. Your mother was killed because she was a liar. A coward. She used her Christian faith to cover up her wrongdoings. She convinced herself she was forgiven just because she cried when she prayed to the God of Heaven, but it doesn't work that way. You must truly repent. You must confess your lies to those you hurt to be forgiven."

"So where is she now? Her soul, I mean?" I asked, but deep down, I already knew the answer.

Onyx let out a subtle laugh, her ruby-colored pupils glistening as she looked me in the eyes.

"Her lying ass went straight to hell."

A part of me felt sadness for my mother. Despite her lies, she had raised me. But she raised me in deception, damaging my spirit in the process. It made sense that God would not accept her in the end. The Bible says you must truly repent to be saved, and she never did that.

"She did it to herself. Every day, the God of Heaven, the Keeper of Spirits, gives his creation the opportunity to do right—to change. He gives us the choice between life and death, right and wrong, blessing and cursing, good and evil. But she chose death, deceit, and darkness. So why should God honor her in death? That is why she died the way she did— marked by a worshipper of Malphas and his earthly wife, Maryan, the gods of the earth."

"Does that mean he is my father? Is that why she never told me the truth about him?" I asked.

"Your earthly father is a worshipper and a son of Malphas. But you asked her many times. And every time, she lied. She manipulated you, played with your emotions as a child, and hindered your growth because of her own selfishness. While she was busy living in deceit, her old enemy was preparing for the perfect time to strike—to complete his powerful ritual."

I had never felt so cold and militant, yet wise and regal. Speaking to my spirit, I felt different—like someone important, someone with wealth and influence.

Looking at Onyx, I saw confidence and certainty. Strength. She was unbreakable, fully aware of who she was. She knew her father. She knew the truth about herself. She knew her bloodline. She was Black royalty if I had ever seen it.

"I want to be like you. I don't want to be broken and sad anymore. I can't go on like this. Help me to be like you, Onyx—my higher self," I said, fighting back the tears of hurt and disappointment.

"You have no idea how long I've waited to hear those words. You are the one who will change our reality. No one—not even our mother—can hold us back now. I will be waiting for you at the ancestral ceremony. Keep the obsidian stone close to your heart. Never take it off. When the time comes, we will become one, walking in awareness, power, and truth. No one will be able to stop us."

The Note

I woke up on the couch, but I didn't remember falling asleep. I didn't even know what time I had passed out.

I looked around for Cheryl, but no one was there. Peering through the blinds, I saw that her black truck was gone.

Slowly getting up, I spotted a handwritten note on the coffee table, addressed to me. Before opening the folded page with my name on it, I thought about last night.

I remembered sitting in the chair across from me, looking through my mother's case file—the one Miss Woods and the mayor had given me. I remembered seeing my mother's face with a different name and background. But the worst part was the picture of her dead body in the morgue. Those images had taken my breath away.

But now, after my dream, the pain felt less sharp.

I thought about my higher self—dark, but fierce and purposeful. She had reminded me why things happened the way they did. Why my mother's life had ended the way it had.

It gave me comfort, knowing that even if my mother had never truly loved me, my spiritual father—though absent—cared for me. One day, he would reveal himself and explain everything.

I had loved my mother. But she was a liar. And how could a person say they love you, raise you, yet lie to your face every single day?

I opened the note…

Ebony,

I'm sorry to leave you like this, but things changed tonight. I spoke with Mayor Goodman, and she told me she's spoken to your mother's family in Virginia. They are very excited to meet you. They are heartbroken over Evelyn and look forward to welcoming you home. Please be open-minded to them.

I've known this family forever, and they are good people. It seems they had nothing to do with your mother's decision to live a lie and disappear from their lives.

Your family is the Bridges, a wealthy and influential family from Old Laketown, Virginia. They are the founders of the first historically Black college, which later became part of Laketown University (LU)—the same school your mother and I attended.

Your aunt, Cassandra Bridges, will be arriving before noon today. So, start packing as soon as you wake up. Don't worry about this house—it will be here whenever you want to visit.

Lastly, this case is officially closed. The Bridges family is bringing in their lawyers and taking over everything. So, I'll be leaving this morning for Old Laketown as well.

Here's my number. Text me if you need anything.

Your friend,

P.I. Cheryl Woods

I smiled. I liked Cheryl. She was a straight shooter. I made sure to save her number because I had a feeling that I would need an honest friend wherever I was going.

Looking up at the clock on the wall, I saw that it was almost 7 AM. That gave me plenty of time to cook my last breakfast in my house and pack my things.

Feeling the cold sensation of the cross against my chest, I suddenly remembered what Onyx had said to me:

"I will be waiting for you at the ancestral ceremony. Keep the obsidian stone close to your heart. Never take it off. And we will become one."

I couldn't wait to meet my family.

I couldn't wait to become the young woman I was destined to be.

The Temple of God's Anointed

A light knock on the door of his private quarters broke the silence the Bishop had enclosed himself in. Ever since the ritual ceremony, he had shunned everyone and everything. Even his assistants had been sent away for the sake of his peace. But he suddenly realized that he had forgotten to lock the door behind him when he returned to his quiet space.

He lay sprawled on his large, deep-brown leather sofa, its golden feet matching the two chairs across from it. The furniture was anchored on top of a plush Persian rug, woven with hues of gold, brown, deep red, and black.

The knock came again, this time a little harder.

He exhaled sharply, suddenly thinking of his wife and how she must be worried about him not coming home. He had called her earlier, but it wasn't like her to disturb his silence. Still, he rose from his slumber and went to answer the door.

"Mrs. Bridges, what a surprise to see you this early morning."

He couldn't take his eyes off the mature woman before him. She looked different from the last time he had laid eyes on her. She stood tall and elegant, reminiscent of her youth. Though her skin bore the grace of time, it remained smooth and well cared for. The maroon-colored dress she wore seemed to flow with an almost supernatural grace as she stepped forward, inviting herself into his quarters.

"Good morning, Holy Bishop. I hope I'm not disturbing your personal worship time, but I came here because we have important matters to attend to," she said with a humble yet alluring smile.

"Do we?" he asked, scrambling through his mind to recall any pre-set appointments for this hour.

"We do," she assured him, standing firm as she waited for him to close the door behind her.

"I see. Well, since you are already in, please refresh my memory. It has been an interesting couple of days," he said as he shut the door and slowly followed her to the seating area.

"Thank you for having a seat, Mrs. Bridges. Can I offer you something to drink? Water, wine, or whiskey, perhaps?"

"No, thank you. I enjoyed a fresh herbal tea on my way to the church this morning."

"So, tell me, what's bothering you, Mrs. Bridges?"

"Bishop, I'll get straight to the point. For as long as I can remember, the women in my family have always served the Dark Lord faithfully. When he decided to step aside, allowing Christian beliefs to become law in this land, we did as instructed. We remained in our lane, assisting where we could. He promised us protection, wealth, and a seat at the table—as long as we supplied him with a worthy sacrifice.

"But it has come to my attention that the last sacrifice— my daughter—was not fulfilled. And that failure has affected me and my great house in more ways than one.

"For years, I have tried to understand why the university has declined, why my health is slowly deteriorating, why my daughter was cursed, why my husband died from a sudden heart attack, and why my son still refuses to return home from war."

"Mrs. Bridges, you can't possibly think—"

"No, Bishop. I now know why my great house has fallen. It is because you and the church did not keep your end of the covenant. You failed us. You did not complete the sacred sacrifice as you were supposed to."

Violet now stood directly in front of Bishop Walter III, her ruby-red eyes glowing with anger.

"Mrs. Bridges, please, I can explain—"

"I know that my court and I have made some mistakes, but we have been working to correct them. I apologize for not coming to you and the Diviner Women sooner, but I didn't want you all to lose faith in me—or worse, in the holy church. We need you. We cannot stand in the sight of our Lord without your power, great wisdom, and influence.

"Mrs. Bridges, you and your sisters are the heart of the Lord. Even today, he still holds you all in high regard because of his wife—your grandmother," the Bishop said, reaching out a pleading hand.

"If you had just come to me, Walter, I would have helped you. My sisters and I would have found her easily and completed the sacrifice. But no… you lost her deep within the Long Pines, didn't you?"

The Bishop slumped back onto his couch, his head buried in his palms in shame.

"Answer me," Violet demanded.

"Yes," he muttered. "We searched everywhere for her. It's as if she just vanished into the forest. I'm so sorry, Great Mother. You have to forgive me."

Violet tilted her head slightly, using her ancestral gift to listen for unseen voices.

She heard nothing.

Curiously, she turned back to him.

"Why are you here alone? I looked—there is no one else here with you. Your aura is dark. Are you depressed? How long have you been in your quarters, Bishop?"

"I… I don't know. Maybe two or three days," he admitted, refusing to meet her gaze. He knew she would see right through him.

"Something is wrong in our community. A darkness is spreading, creating death through pain. I can feel it. Someone is coming for us. I don't know who or why, but we must prepare."

"It's Sheiton. He knows, doesn't he?" she whispered. "He didn't accept your stale sacrifice, did he? He has lost faith in you, hasn't he?"

The Bishop cowered and burst into tears, his sobs echoing in the quiet room.

"I have given up everything for him. I even sacrificed the woman I loved for him. And what has it gotten me? I am nothing without the Sheiton's favor. I'm finished. My father must be turning in his grave. I have disgraced my ancestors."

"Why were we not invited to the completion ritual?" Violet asked, though she already knew the answer.

"I beckoned Sheiton for his help. I knew he would find her and retrieve the heart. But it was too late. Malphas appeared… unhappy. And now, he will return his favor to you, Great Mother. He said the next ruler is coming, and she will be our future."

Violet's eyes narrowed slightly.

"Walter, get yourself together and play your position. Malphas moves in order, and his changes take time. Go home. Love your wife. Be ready when he calls. All is well." She paused. "You are the servant of the god of this world. Hold your head high, no matter what. The people love you—so receive their worship."

The Bishop sniffled, wiping his face. "Thank you, Great Mother. I will take your advice. Be well."

As Violet left the Bishop's quarters, a crooked smile formed on her face, her wicked heart beating faster.

She had received the answer she was looking for—the confirmation she needed.

Elaine Blake was, indeed, her daughter Evelyn.

And her grandchild had been spared—because, somehow, she was favored by Malphas.

She had to meet with her sisters.

Plans had to be made.

Her granddaughter would be the next sacrifice.

It was the only way to restore their power and position—back into their rightful place, in her hands.

CHAPTER TWELVE
THE BISHOP'S LOVE

CHAPTER TWELVE
The Bishop's Love

The Bishop

The Bishop was not prepared to meet with the Great Mother, Violet Bridges. She always had a way of extracting the truth from him. It was her eyes—when they turned into rubies, they made him crumble inside. His emotions were no match for her ancient power. Feeling drained and embarrassed, he started thinking of the only woman he had ever truly loved—her daughter, Evelyn.

He lay back down on his couch, engulfing himself in his happiest memories. The Bishop's father had inherited his grandfather's anointed power shortly after graduating from high school. Because of his father's new position, Walter was granted admission to the prestigious Laketown University—a monumental achievement back in the day. His first couple of years at university were good. He met his girlfriend, now wife, Linda, and they dated for about two years. But everything changed on the first day of his junior year when he locked eyes with Evelyn Bridges.

She was magical. Her smile was bright and warm, lighting up every room she entered. Her reddish-brown hair bounced in effortless curls, and her slim, athletic frame was always impeccably dressed. They had two major things in common: their love for the church and their fascination with history. This ensured they shared at least one class together every semester. Walter found himself constantly staring at Evelyn.

One day, she sat beside him and broke the silence.

"You're Walter, the son of the Holy Bishop, right?"

Walter, stunned that she had even spoken to him, realized he hadn't responded.

"Yeah, that's me. And you're Evelyn, right?"

"Yeah, that's me. So, I noticed that you're always staring at me. Why is that?"

"Oh, I wasn't staring, I was just—"

She raised an eyebrow.

"Okay, you got me," he admitted, smiling nervously. "I guess it's because you're so beautiful, and sometimes I get a little shy."

Evelyn smiled. "I like that you didn't try to deny it but owned it instead. I have a lot of respect for guys who stand in their truth."

"What about you?" Walter asked, intrigued. "Are you an honest person?"

"When I need to be. But I can keep a secret very well," she replied playfully.

For a split second, her eyes flashed deep red. Walter froze. Did he really just see that? He convinced himself he was imagining things. But that was the moment everything changed for him. Whenever he was near Evelyn, his heart melted. He never wanted to leave her side.

Evelyn became his special friend—his forbidden desire. But Linda was the one his father told him to marry. The family was deeply involved in power and politics. Unbeknownst to him, his parents had already arranged his marriage. He had no choice. At the end of his senior year, his father—the Holy Bishop—suffered a heart attack, an event that altered Walter's destiny forever.

For Evelyn, it was the end of her junior year. She had secretly pledged to The Divine Daughters and was chosen for the sacrificial ceremony—the ancient sorority established by the Divine Women of Old Laketown. This was the most powerful group of women, devoted to religiously serving the church and its Holy Bishop.

Evelyn was shocked when she and her friend Wendell saw Walter and his new wife, Linda, holding hands in the church garden, taking wedding photos with photographers. Walter had known that Evelyn and Wendell, a son of Malphas, were getting closer. The night before, when Walter and Evelyn were together, she had confessed her growing feelings for Wendell. But she had also revealed something troubling—Wendell scared her. His personality would shift suddenly. Sometimes, she caught him talking to himself—in a voice that wasn't his.

Walter had wanted to tell her that she was his true love. But he held back. Instead, he told her everything he knew about Wendell—his past, his connections to the church, and Malphas. That night was the last time Walter ever saw her face. Walter knew he couldn't go through with the ceremony when his father revealed the identity of the sacred sacrifice. He pleaded with him to choose another Divine Daughter. But the Divine Mothers had already decided. Then something happened. Evelyn never showed up for the ceremony.

Walter and the church elders searched for her for months. They scoured the entire state of Virginia, believing she had somehow perished in the woods. Shortly afterward, the Holy Bishop died. Walter's world collapsed. In his grief, he turned to God and the church. He poured all his energy into fulfilling his new destiny. He even tried to love his wife. But Linda could never bear him children. So, they adopted a boy from Africa— Myles. He would be the next holy servant of the church. And a loyal son of Malphas, the prince of hell and king of the earth.

Wendell

At midnight, he arrived at the Washington gate. The iron gates opened automatically, allowing him to drive down the long-paved road to his home. The massive cabin stood tall with four levels—three above ground and the largest beneath. His father had built this home after his mother's death. But Wendell made renovations, adding the fourth level for his privacy—and his work. Though his father had been a master builder and a descendant of woodworkers from the Lakely plantation nearly two hundred years ago, Wendell pursued his love of science and the human body.

After a tragic childhood event, he had spent two weeks in a coma. That was when he first met Cain. In the void of unconsciousness, his dark spirit emerged to help him cope with his trauma. Cain spoke to him. And in time, they became one. But when Wendell woke up, so did his fear. Cain was stronger than him. Cain made him do terrible things. He knew he couldn't control him alone. But it was his stepmother who taught him to embrace his truth and accept his duality. Through her mastery of dark magic and worship of Sheiton, she gave him his name. This devotion to the dark lord gave Wendell the strength to control Cain—while still remaining the man he chose to be. But Cain's thirst for vengeance led Wendell down the path of blood rituals. He believed that within blood lay the power to store life—and command death.

After his parents died, Wendell sold half of his father's company. He turned his father's cabins into luxury vacation rentals, partnering with a real estate agency to manage them. This allowed him to continue his stepmother's work—the work of Sheiton and Malphas.

The Washington Mansion

Ten miles outside the Old Laketown neighborhood stands a tall, black wrought-iron gate with intricate patterns resembling intertwined tree branches. This gate is fortified with biometric scanners, a code-entry system, and motion sensors, ensuring that only the invited may enter. Once past the gate, the long driveway winds through dense forest before opening into a circular courtyard paved with smooth stones, featuring an ominous metal sculpture at its center.

Wendell's cabin mansion is a masterpiece of rustic luxury fused with modern sophistication, seamlessly blending into the secluded mountainous landscape. The massive home, originally constructed decades ago by his overambitious father, remains a tribute to his legacy. Out of love and respect for the things his father held dear, Wendell meticulously maintains and enhances the estate.

Nestled among towering, long pine trees, the mansion's dark-stained timber and natural stone exterior make it nearly invisible within the rugged landscape. The steeply pitched roof, covered in slate shingles, offers protection from heavy snowfall and relentless rain. Large floor-to-ceiling windows frame breathtaking views of the vast forest, filling the interior with endless natural light. The house boasts a grand wraparound porch, its handcrafted wooden railing a testament to his father's craftsmanship. The stone fireplace and comfortable seating invite relaxation, perfect for enjoying the crisp mountain air. To the side of the home, a three-car detached garage, aesthetically matched to the mansion, connects via a covered breezeway.

After pulling his truck into the garage, Wendell, consumed by the presence of his dark, corrupt spirit, enters a concealed staircase leading down into the fourth level—a secret basement laboratory and ritual chamber. This hidden sanctum serves as the dwelling place of Cain and his darkest activities.

The laboratory is a stark contrast to the grandeur above. A large industrial fridge lines one wall, housing blood samples meticulously collected from Cain's victims. Each is labeled and stored neatly in glass containers. Wendell retrieves his latest acquisition from the insulated trunk of his truck—a medium-sized cooler preserving fresh blood at an optimal temperature. He methodically transfers the still-warm blood into glass collection tubes, labeling them before placing them alongside the others in the fridge. The body is carefully laid on a human-sized table in the center of the room, wrapped in gauze-like material inside an all-black body bag, waiting to be prepared for the ritual.

A concealed steel door, hidden behind a rotating bookcase in the research area, grants access to the ritual chamber. This space is a world apart from the sterile laboratory, a haunting corridor lined with dim, flickering torches set in iron sconces. The flames cast distorted shadows along the grim stone walls, creating the illusion of movement in the oppressive darkness.

The chamber itself is circular, its walls forged from blackened stone, etched with ancient occult symbols and runes that seem to pulse faintly with an unnatural red glow. The floor, polished obsidian, bears a massive golden pentagram sketched at its center—the heart of all rituals. The thick, heavy air carries a metallic tang of blood, mingled with the intoxicating scent of burning herbs and sacred incense.

At the heart of the chamber stands the altar, an imposing slab of obsidian with sharp, angular edges. The grooves carved into its surface are designed to channel blood, guiding it to its intended purpose. The altar is adorned with sacred ritual tools, each holding dark significance. The Blade of Malphas, the sacrificial dagger, is blackened steel inlaid with golden chalices and encrusted with rubies, its hilt fashioned from ancient, darkened bone—an unholy relic from the depths of hell. Beside it lies the Wand of Sheiton, a relic of immense power, gifted from the underworld itself.

Atop the altar, resting in eerie reverence, is the most prized artifact of all—the Book of Lily, daughter of Mary, The Great Mother. Chosen by Maryan, princess of hell, this ancient spell book is bound in aged black leather, its yellowed pages inscribed in archaic languages and Old English. The journal within contains handwritten notes, diagrams, and incantations chronicling Marianna's journey into the depths of dark worship. For Wendell, this book is an obsession, a relic that draws him ever closer to his stepmother's teachings. Each time he reads it, he hears her voice whispering through the words, guiding him, instructing him.

The towering walls of the chamber rise into a domed ceiling painted with a gruesome scene of hellfire, demonic figures, and tormented souls—a chilling reminder of Wendell's devotion to his dark master. This depiction serves as both an affirmation of his power on earth and a forewarning of the damnation awaiting those who oppose him.

The blood harvest moon looms just days away. Soon, its crimson light will pierce the night sky, and the prince and princess of hell will walk the earth once more. Cain will be ready. The blood of the Divine Daughters, meticulously collected over the last twenty years, will fuel his ritual, restoring his lineage. With diviner blood, he will avenge his mother. He will resurrect his beloved. And when the time comes, his daughter will take her rightful place at his side.

The leaders of Laketown, once so powerful, will bow before him. They will beg for forgiveness for the injustice they allowed. And when they do, Wendell will grant them mercy— or revel in their downfall.

THE DEVIL'S BABY
PART TWO

CHAPTER THIRTEEN
THE LAKETOWN DIVIDE

CHAPTER THIRTEEN
The Laketown Divide

The Revolt of Laketown

In the mid-1800s, Laketown spanned seventy-five acres of plantation land, owned by John and Catherine Lakely. The Lakelys, an English couple, had three children: Cathleen, Cizzy, and John Jr. Devout Christians, John was an ambitious businessman and master carpenter by trade, harboring grand dreams of establishing his own town in America. When the opportunity arose, he seized it. Selling his construction company in England, he purchased land in Virginia, and soon after, twenty enslaved people, whom he forced to work the land, tend the house, and eventually build his envisioned town.

At the time, Virginia was home to numerous plantations, and the arrival of the Lakelys—newcomers from England—piqued the interest of neighboring plantation owners. Eager to solidify his influence, John hosted extravagant dinners, forming alliances with politicians and prominent businessmen. Within five years, his dream materialized. Expanding his team of carpenters, he acquired more enslaved laborers, compelling them to construct Laketown's church, its main road, two stores, two restaurants, a local hotel, and saloons for travelers and entertainment. Alongside his investors, he officially named the settlement Laketown.

The Revolt

Ten years later, in the 1830s, Laketown's prosperity came to a violent halt amid the rising tide of slave revolts sweeping the South. The air was thick with smoke, a stale metallic taste lingered in the mouths of the oppressed, and an insatiable craving for freedom ignited in their hearts. Across the country, enslaved men and women, whether of African descent or Black American Indian lineage, were rebelling against their captors, demanding change. When met with violence—an all-too-common response from slaveholders—the enslaved waited, strategized, and when the time was right, exacted their revenge.

Revolts left blood-stained plantations in their wake. Enslavers and their families were executed in the dead of night, their heads impaled on pikes as symbols of resistance and retribution. Fear had been stripped from the souls of the oppressed purged by their saviors, dark angels who had descended to show them the path to freedom. These celestial beings, Malphas and Maryan, had observed the suffering of the melanated children of the earth for centuries. Since the fall of the great leader Lucifer, the earth and its systems had been left under their dominion. For a hundred years, they had watched as the population of the enslaved outnumbered their oppressors, and so, they listened to their cries, embracing their power, intellect, and rightful dominance over the land.

The Awakening of Mary

Laketown's reckoning began with a horrific crime. A young Black American girl, Kimmy, enslaved on the Lakely plantation, was brutally raped, beaten, and left for dead by visiting white men from town. Kimmy worked in the back of the Lakely Saloon, cooking, cleaning, and doing laundry. As she walked home that evening, she was confronted, attacked, and her unconscious body discarded into the lake bordering Laketown.

That night, Kimmy's mother, Mary, and her sisters waited for her in their small hut on the Lakely plantation, unaware of the horror that had befallen her. By dawn, Kimmy's body was found tangled in tree branches along the shore of the lake, barely alive. Though conscious, she was weak—battered and broken. The moment her mother arrived and saw her, Mary's soul shattered. She screamed into the sky, her cries reaching beyond the earth as she begged for divine intervention. The elder women of the plantation gathered, joining in desperate prayer, but as Kimmy's life continued to slip away, Mary's faith crumbled.

"Where is this God?" Mary wailed. "Where is His healing power? His protection for our children? Why do we pray to a God who does not see us? Who lets us suffer at the hands of the white man every day?"

An elder, attempting to console her, gently responded, "Have faith, daughter. God hears you. The Bible says—"

"The Bible?" Mary's voice was sharp with fury. "What has this Bible done for us? It was forced upon us to make us slaves. This God is not our friend. He is not our savior. He is their God. And their God has abandoned us."

The elder mother's wrinkled hands trembled as she reached for Mary, whispering, "The Bible is all that we have… Please, don't give up on it now. God will never leave you nor forsake you."

Mary fell silent. Then, her expression hardened. She turned to her four daughters—Vivian, Marie, Rose, and Etta—and took their hands.

"Yes, Elder Mother, I will seek the scriptures. For it says—seek, and you shall find."

She then recited an ancient chant—one whispered through generations of enslaved women who refused to surrender their faith to their captors' religion. Her words were old, yet powerful, invoking the spirits of those who had suffered before her. She called not upon the God of their oppressors but upon the God of Power. Her voice wove together scripture and ancestral knowledge, summoning forces beyond the reach of men.

For nearly an hour, she chanted, and her daughters repeated in unison.

"For the savior of my enemies is not my savior. But the enemy of their God is my God."

Then, the sky split open.

A lightning bolt struck the shore, igniting a fire that burned without spreading. The elder mothers fled in terror, but Mary and her daughters stood firm. They had no fear left to give.

A figure emerged through the flames, time itself seeming to halt. She was ethereal—tall, dark, commanding. Her presence swallowed the air itself. Her name was Maryan, wife of Malphas, prince of hell, daughter of Sheiton, the Dark Lord.

She gazed upon Mary with piercing ruby-red eyes, then reached out, clasping Mary's trembling hands. Her voice, deep and melodic, echoed through the night.

"I have come to do his bidding. He has seen your pain. He has heard your cries. For centuries, we have waited, watching, to see if His all-powerful father in heaven would grant you favor. But He has not."

Mary's breathing quickened as Maryan continued, "Sheiton, the first of his kind, once the most favored of his creator, will show you true power. He will protect you."

The dark angel's grip tightened. "Mary, because you have chosen to believe in something greater, you will be my daughter. Your bloodline will be blessed with divine power. But to prove your devotion, you must make the ultimate sacrifice. Are you willing? Are you ready to lead your people to freedom?"

Mary swallowed the lump in her throat. She looked down at Kimmy, then at her four living daughters. Her hand rested on her womb, where another daughter stirred. Her voice did not waver.

"Yes, Dark Angel Maryan. I am willing. I am ready. I will do whatever it takes to protect my daughters and my people."

Maryan smiled, then knelt beside Kimmy, lifting her frail body with ease. She drew a golden blade, its edge gleaming ominously under the blood moon, and with a single stroke, slit Kimmy's throat.

Gasps filled the air, but Mary did not move. She did not weep.

Maryan filled a golden chalice with Kimmy's blood, then, slicing her own palm, allowed her own immortal blood to mix within. She handed the chalice to Mary.

"Drink, and you shall be reborn."

With steady hands, Mary drank. Her daughters followed, one by one, sealing their fates.

Maryan lifted the chalice skyward, chanting the ancestral words once more. As the blood poured over them, their transformation began.

Ruby-red eyes flashed in the darkness. Power surged through their veins. The Divine Women were born.

And that night, Laketown burned.

Old Laketown

By sunrise the next morning, every plantation owner, businessman, lawman, and investor in Laketown was dead—along with their families. Heads were staked in front of homes and lined the roads leading into town, a warning to all who dared to oppose the revolt. The uprising spread swiftly, igniting plantations across Virginia, leaving them engulfed in flames. A few plantation owners managed to escape, seeking aid, but the stories of the Great Mother and her power spread faster than they could flee. When outsiders came to see the aftermath for themselves, they were met with the overwhelming stench of death and the sight of decapitated heads—a grim display of justice.

Freed from their oppressors, the formerly enslaved took control of Laketown. They reclaimed the land they had cultivated and, to honor their past, named the heart of their community Old Laketown. They vowed never to forget the old ways. Their numbers grew from fifty to over three hundred, including women and children. Among them were skilled farmers, herbalists, carpenters, and craftsmen. Under the guidance of the Great Mother and her communion with the dark lord, they established leaders, built homes, and reopened businesses, welcoming black travelers and the formerly enslaved into their thriving town.

As America solidified itself as a Christian nation, the leaders of Old Laketown concealed their true beliefs and identities. They spent a decade constructing a grand cathedral, the Temple of God's Anointed, adopting the appearance of Christian faith to maintain peace and prosperity. This allowed them to conduct business beyond their borders while still holding dominion over their land. When the Emancipation Proclamation was signed years later, Old Laketown leaders permitted descendants from other plantations to settle in Laketown. To the outside world, Laketown was a historic town honoring the resilience of the formerly enslaved. But an unspoken rule remained—no one was to interfere with the Old Laketown community. Those who did quickly learned why the past should never be disturbed.

The doorbell rang at the Bridges estate, and Mason, the family butler, answered with his usual professionalism.

"Good morning, sisters. The Great Mother is expecting you in the family study. May I take your coats?"

"Thank you, Mason," they responded, handing him their mink and faux fur coats.

Once inside, one of the sisters reached for the old slave Bible placed at the end of the mantle. The moment she touched it, a hidden door within the walls unlocked. The grand stairwell beyond was lined with black candles, leading them into a sacred underground sanctuary—the original church of Old Laketown. Built by their ancestors over a century and a half ago, it remained untouched by time.

The walls bore sacred altars, each adorned with hand-painted portraits of past Great Mothers and powerful sisters. Herbs, crystals, offerings, and flickering black candles surrounded them, their flames dancing alongside the burning incense. The sanctuary itself was simple but meticulously preserved—a space the size of a modern-day basement, its floors crafted from pinewood harvested by their forefathers.

Twelve pews, six on each side, led to a raised pulpit with an all-black cross painted on its face. The pews bore matching black crosses at their ends. Small, screened windows allowed in faint traces of daylight, but the church's entrance was nailed shut. The only way in or out was through the Bridges estate, ensuring the secrecy of their gatherings.

The divine women—the direct descendants of the Great Mother Mary—were now grandmothers, each carrying the ancient power of their bloodline, passed down to a chosen daughter in every generation. Violet, "the voice," was the eldest. Her lineage possessed the gift of the voice—a power that could cast spells through speech and song, heal pain, and inspire courage. As the matriarch, Violet used her melodic gifts to unite her sisters and uplift Old Laketown. She had married Robert Bridges III, a master carpenter and architect, who rebuilt the Old Laketown bridge that connected the community to the main town.

Next was Mae, "the skyshaper." Her bloodline could command the elements—summoning storms, calming winds, and calling the rain to nourish and protect the land. She used her abilities to ensure the safety and prosperity of Old Laketown. Mae had married Lee Allen and had four children.

Olivia, "the lovekeeper," carried the power of attraction—drawing wealth, success, and deep connection. She could cleanse money of negative energy, turning small investments into fortune. She used her abilities to bless the businesses of Old Laketown and strengthen relationships within the community. Olivia married Winston Parker and had three children.

Etta, "the oathbinder," had a bloodline gifted in truth and justice. Her abilities allowed her to dismantle corruption, sway court rulings, and reveal hidden motives. She was a natural protector, ensuring fairness within Old Laketown. Etta had married Edward Moore and had two children.

The youngest was Lilian, "the warden." Her bloodline had the ability to commune with spirits, guide souls to the afterlife, and harness the wisdom of the dead. Her power was not about fearing death but understanding and respecting it. She used her gift to provide closure to those grieving in Old Laketown. Lilian had married Will Turner and had two sets of twins—one pair of identical girls, the other identical boys.

The Gathering

"Sisters, you made it. Thank you for coming on such short notice," Violet greeted them with a warm but serious smile as they entered the sacred space.

"Very short notice," Mae scoffed. "I had to cut my vacation short for this, so it better be good."

"Says the one who would complain if I didn't invite her," Violet teased.

"Alright then, out with it," Anita chimed in. "We haven't had any good gossip in years."

"It must be serious if you sounded that demanding over the phone, Vee," Lilian added, sipping a glass of red wine she had brought with her.

"Lili, did you even think to bring a bottle for the rest of us?" Olivia scolded.

"Excuse the hell out of me," Lilian shot back. "I didn't hear you ask for anything."

"Sisters, please," Violet interrupted, raising a hand to silence them. "I need you all to listen. Change is coming, and we must prepare."

"Change?" The room stilled.

Violet inhaled deeply before speaking. "Twenty years ago, my heir was chosen as the sacred sacrifice to our dark mother, Maryan. But the ritual was never completed. The Holy Bishop failed us."

A murmur of disbelief spread through the room.

"What do you mean?" Mae's face darkened. "Have you been living under a curse all this time?"

"Yes," Violet confirmed. "And unknowingly, so has Old Laketown."

"What in the hell—" Olivia clenched her fists. "That weak bastard didn't even invite us to the ceremony, did he?"

"No," Violet said grimly. "He confessed to me—then cried about it like a child."

"I never liked him," Mae snapped. "I told you all when he was born that he would be worthless."

Violet nodded. "But today, there is good news, sisters. Sheiton has returned to us. A ram in the bush has been revealed."

The air in the room shifted.

"Our power will be restored."

"What ram?" Lilian asked.

Violet's lips curled into a smile. "Evelyn had a daughter."

The sisters gasped.

"Her name is Ebony."

Silence fell over the room.

"She is coming here tonight. She turns eighteen tomorrow. Under the blood harvest moon, we will complete the sacred ritual."

Olivia exhaled sharply. "So our power will live on."

"Yes," Violet confirmed. "And with Maryan's blessing, we will return to our rightful place."

Mae placed a hand over her heart. "Sisters, do we all agree?"

"In unity," they whispered, bowing their heads in prayer to the dark princess.

And so, preparations began. Ebony's fate had been sealed.

CHAPTER FOURTEEN
THE ROAD TO LAKETOWN

CHAPTER FOURTEEN
The Road to Laketown

Ebony

Driving with Aunt Cassandra to Virginia has been the most fun I've had in weeks, maybe even months. It's like I'm living in a fantasy novel that I never want to wake up from. My left arm is sore because I keep punching it to make sure I'm really alive. All of my young life, I dreamed of moments like this—to see family members who look like me, to have someone call my name and expect me to answer. I remember one Christmas in the fifth grade, my teacher, Mrs. Crabtree, tried so hard to keep my spirits up for the holiday play. When she asked about my dad and if I knew him, I told her, "Miss Crabtree, I don't have a daddy. Whoever he is, he doesn't love me, just like the rest of my family." That evening, she had her whole family come out to cheer for me at the play. They waited to take pictures with me and my mom afterward. That was the first time I had ever felt loved by someone other than my mother. And yet, my mama didn't shed one tear. She knew all along who she was, who I was, and how much this would have meant to me—but she didn't care.

Now here I am, riding for hours in this nice truck with a woman who is my real aunt. I can't believe it. My mother must have really hated me, or her own family, to keep such a lie from me for my whole life.

I have an Aunt Cassandra. I look at her with amazement because she is absolutely gorgeous. I catch myself staring at her all the time. I know she can feel my eyes on her, but I just can't stop taking it all in. From the moment my phone rang until now, it's all been surreal.

After reading Miss Cheryl's note, I decided to make a nice breakfast for myself, clean up the kitchen, and begin packing. Sitting in the kitchen, looking around, brought back so many memories. My whole life was created in that house. Now that Mama is gone and so much has been revealed, I actually look forward to something new. But as excitement bubbles inside me, a wave of overwhelm creeps up my spine, tightening my shoulders and neck. I have to sit down and just breathe. As I start to relax, my spirit speaks to me. In a trance, I feel my body float toward the darker version of me. She reaches for my hands, her glowing ruby-red eyes locking onto mine.

"You can do this. You are called to greatness," she says, her voice steady and powerful. "Don't overthink the packing process. Change your perspective. Pack your bags like you're going on a month-long trip. Take what's important. And just know, this house is yours. You can always come back."

As I blink, I find myself back in my chair, my mind clear. Moving in my own flow, I finish packing, ready to meet my long-lost family. Just as I zip my last bag, my cell phone rings. It's Charlotte. We haven't spoken in a while. She went on a trip with her dad shortly after my mom died. Thinking about it now, it was probably her mother, the mayor, who sent her away—to keep her from me, to protect her. But honestly, I can't be mad. The mayor helped me more than anyone.

"Hey, Char, how are you?"

"Hey, Eb, how you been holding up? My mom said she found your long-lost family. Girl, when she sat me down and told me, I screamed."

"Aww, Char—"

"No, Ebony, you know I am the one person who knows how much this means to you," Charlotte replies, her voice shaking with tears.

"Girl, honestly, I don't know how to feel. These last few weeks have been like I'm living in a fantasy novel."

"I know, right? More like a suspense thriller!"

"I know, right? One minute I have a mama and no family, and now I have a family but no mama."

"Girl, somebody wake me up! 'Cause this shit ain't funny no more."

"Well, Eb, what you gonna do now?"

"I'm all packed up, ready to go to a new place to meet my new family. And maybe one day soon, I'll meet the father I never knew."

"Girl, this could definitely be a movie."

"You know you have to tell me all the crazy details."

"But seriously, Charlotte, your mom has been so kind to me. Almost like another mother I never knew I had." My voice breaks as tears roll down my face. "I honestly don't know where I'd be if it wasn't for her and her team."

"Aww, that means so much to me and my family. Before my dad and I left on the fishing trip, I made her promise she'd help you before I left for Spelman."

"Really, Charlotte? Well, just know she kept her promise, bestie."

"So guess what? I'm meeting my real family at noon. My Aunt Cassandra is coming to pick me up and take me to Laketown, Virginia. Can you believe it? All this time, I had a whole family in another state."

Charlotte gets quiet. I can hear her breathing, but she doesn't answer right away.

"Ebony, you know I love you. I've always tried to stay out of drama about your mama, but girl, I have to speak my truth."

I brace myself. Charlotte never holds back.

"I hear things, Eb. And your mama was always being talked about. There were people in this town who knew her— maybe even her family. She had a reputation for lying and conning folks. Just like she lied to you, she might have lied to your real dad too."

"Damn, Char. Anything else you wanna get off your chest about my mama?"

"I'm sorry. I just want you to be prepared. If you do meet your father, be patient. He might not even know you exist."

I go quiet. I don't know what to say. But she could be right. Charlotte always makes me see things differently.

"And there you go again with that hardcore Charlotte wisdom. Even though what you're saying hurts, you could be right. I appreciate you, bestie. I love you so much."

"Okay, girl. Go meet your family. You know I'll always be here for you. Let's stay in touch and let me know what college you pick."

"Always and forever, bestie."

As soon as I hang up, there's a knock at the front door. When I open it, the most beautiful Black woman stands before me. She has long, straight black hair with reddish-brown roots, smooth peanut butter skin, and a floral perfume that floats in with the breeze. She smiles, showing bright white teeth just like my mother's.

"Hi, you must be my only niece, Ebony."

I freeze. The rush of emotions overwhelms me. My heart takes over my mind, and all I can do is cry happy tears and smile. I want to run to her and say how much I love her, how much I've longed for her. But fear and uncertainty hold me still.

Seeing my hesitation, she reaches for me, pulling me into the biggest hug of my life. Our heartbeats sync in a steady rhythm, our blood recognizing each other.

Aunt Cassandra looks into my eyes and says, "Ebony, there's so much I want to say, but my heart is so full. I have so many questions."

"I know, and I'm so sorry."

"Sorry? What do you have to be sorry for?"

"For not knowing you existed."

She pulls me closer. "We'll get to the bottom of everything. But for now, let's take it one day at a time, okay?"

I nod, knowing for the first time in my life—I'm not alone.

***

"Shit, honey, you good? I'm sorry I didn't mean to wake you. I just spilled this hot coffee on my pants."

"Where are we?"

"About ten miles outside of Laketown. I stopped to get some gas and a fresh cup of coffee. But I guess I didn't seal the top all the way. I hate it when I do that."

"That's funny, Mama used to do the same thing. Some mornings when she would take me to school, she'd always have her coffee with her, but when she hit bumps along the dirt road, she would say the same thing."

"Really? That is kinda funny. Evelyn always had a dirty mouth. She would be the first one out of all of us to get in trouble for talking trash."

"Yep, that sounds like her. Always had something to say."

"Okay and didn't nobody ask her for it either. Oh, but she was gonna give it though."

"Just couldn't keep it to herself."

We both took a few minutes to laugh, but then things got kinda sad all over again. Aunt Cassandra looked away out of her window that faced the gas station pumps and wiped her face.

"Ebony, I wished she would have just called me. Just reached out to me for help. You know, that's the part that hurts me the most. The fact that she felt she couldn't trust me."

"You know, Aunt Cassandra, all my life I felt that I was born with a yearning for family. Millions of times I cried to my mother. Even when I tried to move on and turn it off, my heart just wouldn't let me."

"Really."

"But you know what? Ever since I can remember, Mama lied. She would make up stories. She would say how God took y'all away. She had all types of tales that she told me. But never the truth. Never."

"That's so crazy to me. That she went her whole life lying and deceiving, only for it to end in such a horrific way."

"I'm so sorry, Ebony, but I'm mad. I'm mad as hell."

"Me too, Auntie. I'm past being sad. Now I'm just pissed."

"I'm mad at my mother for being a liar, and I'm mad at the person who went out of their way to take her from me. Now I'll never get to confront her and demand the truth. Because I want to know everything. I deserve to know."

"Yeah, well, sometimes you think you know your parents, and then something traumatic happens, and they turn into this dark mystical creature right in front of you. Then everything that you thought was, isn't. You know what I mean?"

Looking at Aunt Cassandra's face in the rearview mirror and listening to her intense words sparked my left eyebrow to raise. I see I'm not the only one who has recently been through some type of crazy trauma. She must be talking about Grandma.

"Auntie, all I can say about that is, nothing in my life is real to me anymore. Ever since Mama was killed, every day I wake up, there's something new for me to learn or understand. I told my best friend it's like I'm living in a fantasy novel, for real."

"Oh, niece, it's definitely some type of horror or even a thriller for sure."

Laketown Revealed

"Well, welcome to Laketown, Virginia, niece, the last part of your fantastical story. This small city is full of so much history, it's crazy."

"That's amazing because I love history."

"Really? That's great because I love sharing the history of my city."

"Please, Auntie, tell me all about it."

"Well, to be honest, Laketown has changed a lot over the recent years due to modernization and an increase in technology. It's not like New York or Los Angeles, but we have a lot of upgrades, and the city is very clean."

"I've never been to those big cities, but I've seen them on TV."

"Okay, well, in Laketown, there is one set of highways that take you north and south of the city. There is one set of main roads that can take you east and west, which you can reach from the highway or take back roads. The downtown area is full of culture and historic statues with smooth paved roads that cater to tourists. Laketown is known for its southern food cuisine and fresh seafood that comes from Freedman's Lake, which is our largest body of water that frames the land. We have a very big fresh market where the local merchants have been selling their goods for over a hundred years."

"Oh, my goodness, Auntie, you have to take me there sometime. I'd like to see that."

"Okay, the fresh market is every other Saturday, so at least twice a month, but sometimes depending on how the days fall in the month, it could be three times."

"We also have some historic churches that have been around for almost a hundred years, but the oldest church is our church, where our family members have served for well over a century, The Temple of God Anointed, led by our holy bishop. He also presides over all the other churches within the region."

"Oh, your church sounds big. Is it like those mega churches you see on Sunday morning TV?"

"I guess so. We have about ten thousand members. The services are held twice on Sundays and midweek services on Wednesdays and Thursdays."

It was so nice driving through the city of Laketown. We arrived late afternoon, so there was some evening traffic that Aunt Cassandra did not appreciate, but I loved every minute of it. It just gave me more time to really take it all in. The buildings downtown were tall and metallic looking. The windows looked like glass mirrors that shined bright in the afternoon sun. The city lights were bright, and the streets were filled with people out walking. Some were shopping at the local stores and department stores, and others were enjoying late lunches and early dinners under the different colored terrace umbrellas. As we drove south of the city, there were more homes and communities that catered to the city folks. Aunt Cassandra said that she used to live in that area years ago, but recently moved back in with Grandma Violet. Which is good to know because it looks like we will all be living in the same house together.

Aunt Cassandra pulled over to the side as we approached a wooden bridge that looked old yet restored to have a modern historic feel to it.

"Let's get out and stretch a bit. I want to show you something very special."

"Okay, I could use a good stretch."

The beautiful forest trees came alive as the gentle leaves danced with the blowing of cool wind through the towering pine trees. This land felt different. Walking, I felt a sense of purpose and a feeling that I belonged here somehow.

"This place is something very special that I wanted to share with you, niece. And by the way, I keep calling you that because a couple days ago, I had never had a niece or nephew, and now I have you. I'm so happy to have you, Ebony."

"Thank you, Auntie. I can't stress enough how much of a dream come true it is to have you, too."

Here you go ahead and read the short story of the lake," she said as she stepped aside for me to read out loud for both of us to hear. On a large wooden sign near the edge of the lake, weathered by time yet still standing firm, Freedmen's Lake, it read in large letters, with a small inscription below that told of its origins.

"*Over two hundred and fifty years ago, the black enslaved tried everything to escape the horrors of chattel slavery. Searching for their freedom, some jumped, some dove, and others were thrown into this large body of water. All were washed away in its deadly tides filled with large sharp stones that sit at its bottom. The plantation masters used this lake to capture their prey and tortured their slaves for years. Once the slaves were freed, their children, who established the great town of Laketown, named this lake Freedmen's Lake to commemorate this sacred body of water, their ancestors, and their remains.*"

Taking a deep breath as I stood there, I felt a deep connection to this place. It reminded me of the dark history of this country that seems to haunt Black people no matter where we go. It also symbolized the beauty of survival that came long after the horrors we had endured as a people.

"You see, niece, Freedmen's Lake is not just a lake; it is a testament to the strength of those that came before us, a place where the past and present intertwine in a melody of reverence and remembrance."

"Auntie, I've never felt this way before. What is this, this feeling?"

"Ebony, this is the beginning of you understanding the deep connection of family and community. This place here is your true home. Now, let me show you the next best thing at this spot, the bridge."

As I walked further toward the bridge, I could see the mountains in the close distance as Freedmen's Lake shimmered. The water's surface rippled at a rhythm, as if nature itself remembered and mourned the stories it held. The lake framed the rolling hills and peaks of the nearby mountains, their white snowy caps catching the sunlight and casting golden reflections on the water.

"This oldie but goodie is a precious jewel and also our family's heirloom that we share with the citizens of Laketown and Old Laketown. This bridge was originally built by your great-great-grandfather, Robert Bridges I. Great-grandfather Robert was a slave who helped build the town of Laketown, which centuries ago was all a plantation called the Lakely Plantation."

"Really? How did he do it?"

"Well, many say he was empowered by dark magic that helped to free the slaves and, most of all, kept them safe from their enemies who were burning down strong Black towns all across the country."

"Aunt Cassandra, is dark magic real?"

"Ebony, I know it sounds crazy, but yes, it is very real. Just like our religion is real because of our belief in it, the same applies to magic. Because we believe in its power, we give it the essence to exist in this earthly realm."

"I haven't told anyone this, but over the last week, I have experienced a strong dark spirit within me. She speaks to me and has been a comfort to my soul. Why is that?"

"It's the power that lies within our bloodline, niece. It's passed down to the chosen by our ancestors who toiled on this earth, and because of their sacrifice for life and freedom, we stand here anointed by the sacred blood today."

"You said Great-Grandfather Robert was chosen too?"

"Yes, he was one of the originals—the slaves of the great revolt of the Lakely Plantation. Days after the Great Mother's sacrifice, the people of the plantation were all blessed by the dark lord."

"Who is the dark lord, Auntie?"

"He has many names. The elders call him The Morning Star because he sat at the right hand of the God of heaven and helped lead heaven for millions of years. His bones were made of the purest diamonds, and his body was of pure gold. He glistened in the rays of the sun, which is how he received his name. But his love and dedication to his father turned to jealousy when the God of heaven started to create man from this planet and formed him in his image."

"But why is he the dark lord of man if he doesn't like us?"

"That's a good question, niece. I was told by my mentor that after Morning Star's great fall, he took half of the heavenly host with him into Hades, or Hell, which the ancestors called the dark realm. There, he became the dark lord, filled with hate and sadness for his father. But his skills as a leader became even more powerful, and he eventually battled with God's youngest son on earth. The dark lord won that battle and became the great ruler of this realm and all the power systems and structures within it. His pure golden outer form transformed into the sacred black obsidian stone, but his diamond skeletal bones remain untouched, another source of his power."

"The obsidian stone—you mean this stone?" I reached for my sacred cross, which I kept hidden around my neck.

"Yes, how did you— Where did you get this?"

"I found this within a sacred journal that Mama clearly left for me. I think she was going to give it to me on my eighteenth birthday because she left me a note inside it."

"Of course, she had the missing Diviner Journal this whole time. The family counted it lost, but you are the one, Ebony, who's going to make everything right again."

"Come on, let's get going. I can't wait for you to meet my mother, your grandmother, the now Great Mother, Violet Bridges, the matriarch of our family."

"Man, when you say it like that, I feel kinda nervous. Do you think she'll like me?"

"Oh, honey, she already loves you and is overjoyed that she even has a granddaughter."

Aunt Cassandra's face went dim, and we walked back to the truck. Her eyes became blank and cold, like her thoughts were reflecting on a past that was once alive but now dead.

"Auntie, are you okay? I'm sorry if I upset you. Sometimes I can ask too many questions."

"No, niece, it's not you. Really, it's just—I recently divorced my husband and lost our set of twins in an abusive marriage. He beat me so badly one night—the last night I can remember—I was carrying my babies inside my womb, and when I woke up in the hospital, they were gone. The doctors said I had lost so much blood that they died inside me and had to be removed."

I sat in the truck, unable to move. Then I remembered to breathe.

"Oh my God, that is the worst. I can't imagine the hate you must have in your heart for him. How have you been able to move on from such pain?"

"I couldn't on my own. But my doctor, who is a good friend of mine, referred me to a healing facility that focused on mental and spiritual healing. I was sent away for about a year and a half, then eventually came back and started working with my family and community in the Old Laketown building at the university. I sold our house and moved back in with my mother permanently. I'll be there forever, I'm sure of it."

"Oh, Auntie, I'm so, so, so sorry."

"Me too, niece, me too."

After some more time of tears, tight hugs, and precious bonding, Aunt Cassandra started the truck, and we took our time driving across the historical rustic-style bridge.

After some more time of tears, tight hugs, and precious bonding, Aunt Cassandra started the truck, and we took our time driving across the big historical rustic-style bridge. Hand-carved images of people, whom I learned were my ancestors and other influential town leaders, adorned its structure. The deep red wooden beams accentuated its historic essence, while the massive copper-colored supports reflected its modern yet industrial edge. The matte black roof stood fifteen to sixteen feet tall and twenty-four feet wide, ensuring proper clearance for all vehicles. The lower interior on both sides was built of red brick, with low-level lighting that illuminated the built-in sidewalk for those daring enough to cross over Freedmen's Lake.

The Old Laketown Community

As we crossed over the bridge, maintaining the speed limit of forty-five miles per hour, we approached a four-way traffic light that revealed something truly breathtaking. I sat up in the back seat of Aunt Cassandra's Range Rover, realizing that the Old Laketown community was a large neighborhood nestled atop a Virginia mountain. This was the most beautiful place I had ever seen in my entire life. At the light, there was a nicely paved highway that led left or right, but going straight ahead would take us into the fiercely preserved community of Old Laketown. The light could not turn green fast enough.

Aunt Cassandra glanced at me and smiled. I must have looked like a child entering Disney World for the first time. My heart raced. I couldn't sit back in my seat, afraid I might miss something or someone. The red brick road that started at the beginning of the bridge continued as soon as we crossed the paved highway. Old Laketown took my breath away.

Beautiful Black people in all shades were everywhere. They walked along the sidewalks, drove luxurious cars and trucks, and shopped at neighborhood stores. Families and friends dined at local restaurants, their laughter filling the streets. I let my window down to take it all in. As we entered Old Laketown, we approached the Old Laketown sign, which sat in the middle of a roundabout leading in three different directions.

"So this is Old Laketown," Aunt Cassandra said. "Our community, built, preserved, and rebuilt over the years. Our ancestors decided long ago to reclaim the place that caused their suffering and transform it into something beautiful. They left this sacred place for us, and we have learned to take that responsibility very seriously."

"Auntie, I have never seen a place so beautiful and magical in my life. Where should we go first?"

"Well, if you take the exit to the right, which the sign says is west, you'd go down Temple Road. If you stay on this roundabout and head north, you'll go down Old Laketown Road. But if you take the roundabout and veer slightly right, you'll turn onto Cherry Street."

"Aunt Cassandra, do you smell that? It smells like fresh baked bread and donuts."

"Oh yes, honey, that's Miss Juanita's Bakery. She starts baking her goods around five o'clock in the morning. I stop by at least once a week. Miss Juanita's Bakery has been around for over a hundred years. Her great-grandmother was the master baker on the old Lakely Plantation, and after she was freed and blessed by the Great Mother, she used her skills to start her own business. The community supported her, and now her descendants continue to bless us with their ancestral gifts. They use fresh herbs and homegrown ingredients in everything they make. We get our baked goods, cakes, fresh breads, and yes, even donuts from their family business."

"That's amazing. I love how everything looks on this road."

"Yes, this is Old Laketown Road. It's about three and a half miles long and was the first road ever built on this side of Lakely Mountain. Of course, it was built by the slaves, so once they were freed, they decided to preserve the red brick and expand upon it. Our forefathers were master builders of this great community, and our family has been the keepers of its history. You'll see that Grandma Violet takes that responsibility very seriously."

"So this road that we are driving on right now is over two hundred years old?"

"Yes."

"Oh my God. I've never known anything this old—except maybe the trees. And look at these trees, how they hover over us, lining the entire street."

Ancient oak trees towered over the majestic scenery, their branches draped in cascading veils of Spanish moss. The thick, gnarled limbs crisscrossed overhead, forming a natural archway that filtered sunlight, creating dappled patterns across the brick road and sidewalks. A late afternoon breeze gently swayed the moss, adding a sense of mystery to this enchanting environment. I could only imagine the countless stories these timeless great oaks had witnessed throughout the centuries. Their presence set the tone of elegance and historic Victorian charm that resonated throughout the whole community.

The sidewalks were paved with the same aged red brick, slightly uneven with hints of moss growing in the cracks, adding to the historic vibe. Neat rows of flowerbeds burst with vibrant azaleas, their bright pinks and whites contrasting against the deep greens of the mossy oak trees. Gas-styled lanterns, with weathered iron frames, stood along the sidewalks, their flickering light enhancing Old Laketown's Victorian charm.

Behind the trees, rows of stately Victorian-styled red brick buildings lined both sides of the road. The ground floors housed charming local businesses, their large bay windows displaying their services. Above, the second, third, and fourth floors were residential apartments, marked by shuttered windows and hanging plants spilling over balcony railings.

Aunt Cassandra took her time driving me through her favorite part of the community, pointing out businesses, their history, and the people who ran them. But I could not take my eyes off the biggest building at the end of the road—the Old Laketown Clubhouse, formerly known as the Lakely Plantation House, or as Aunt Cassandra called it, The Big House.

"Okay, our last stop before we head home to meet Grandma Violet is The Big House—aka, the Old Laketown Clubhouse. Very well-preserved in its original Victorian style, this was the place where everything started for us as a community. Our ancestors chose to keep it after the Great Revolt of the early eighteen hundreds and maintained the Victorian theme throughout the entire community."

"Oh, that's why all the roads are made of red brick, and the community has that elegant southern charm to it."

"Exactly, and we are very proud of that."

Aunt Cassandra parked in front of the old Victorian mansion and gave me a brief description of the exterior, promising to bring me back later for a full tour.

We then drove further down the street, turning left into a section of the community called Laketown Charm. This was where the most beautiful Victorian southern homes were, and they weren't far from the clubhouse. The lots were massive, each home an architectural masterpiece. But the house we pulled up to was one of the biggest on Cherry Street.

The Bridges Mansion

We turned onto a winding cobblestone driveway lined with moss-covered low stone walls, dotted with wrought-iron lamp posts flickering in the evening light. The mansion was a dark gothic Victorian masterpiece, exuding an aura of mysticism and power. Painted a rich obsidian black, its gold accents gleamed like firelight against its dark backdrop, giving it an almost magical glow as the evening sun hit it.

The steep mansard roof was crowned with a domed turret, its golden trim faintly glowing in the dimming sky. Tall chimneys rose elegantly against the backdrop of the surrounding forest. Stained-glass windows glowed amber from the warm lights within, giving the mansion an ethereal presence.

Aunt Cassandra parked the Range in the circular driveway. The front door was adorned with a detailed iron gate with swirling designs, flanked by gaslit lanterns that cast flickering shadows on the stone steps leading up to the entrance.

A beautifully mature woman with silver hair pulled into a thick braid resting on her shoulder opened the front door as we got out of the truck. When I looked up at her, I saw my mother's face. The same complexion. The same exact smile. And when she spoke, she sounded just like Mama. I dropped my bag, and before I could say anything, tears streamed down my face. She descended the steps, cupped my face in her hands, and looked directly into my eyes, searching my soul. Then she smiled and said words that changed me forever: "Welcome home, Ebony Bridges."

Ebony Bridges. It had a nice ring to it. I think I'll keep it.

THE KILLING

CHAPTER FIFTEEN
The Killing

As Cheryl parked her Tahoe in the lot of the McDillion police station, she thought she heard something shift in her trunk. It was packed with various items—old boxes from home, a suitcase full of clothes, personal belongings, and materials related to her case. When she opened the trunk, one of the bags tumbled out. As she picked up the fallen items, she noticed something she didn't remember packing: an old box labeled with her father's name and his last case—D. Travis/Diviner Case.

Her eyes moved side to side in deep reflection. She was certain she hadn't put that box there. Then, a quick smile appeared on her face as she recalled her mother helping her pack before she left. Her mama must have slipped it in among the other boxes and bags. There was no other explanation. Still, it was her dad's box, and she had thought she had seen all of them—or so she believed.

Cheryl glanced around the parking lot. The bright lights illuminated the area, but there was no one near her truck. She only saw other officers entering the side doors of the building. From the looks of it, they were the team from the second killing, bringing in evidence for Detective James. She hesitated for a second, debating whether to wait and look through the mysterious box later. But something inside her urged her on. She needed to see what was inside. She grabbed the box and pulled it closer. As she stood at the trunk's edge, the bottom of the box suddenly gave out, sending its contents spilling onto the ground.

"What the—?" she muttered in frustration.

It must have been old and rotted. As she gathered the papers and photos, her breath caught in her throat. There, staring back at her, were pictures of her father, Donald Travis. His lifeless body lay in the woods, throat slit, his skin pale gray—drained of all his blood. Cheryl froze. She had always known her father had been murdered, but she had never known exactly how. Her mother had never spoken about it.

It had been over twenty years since she and her mother, Mary, had lost him. Yet, the pain still felt raw, as if it had happened yesterday. She flipped through more of the paperwork, uncovering pictures of the young women from her father's last case—the Divine Daughters. The images showed the victims with their throats cut, wrists slit in the shape of crosses, their bodies completely drained of blood. The reports stated that their remains had been found deep in the woods outside the Old Laketown community.

This couldn't be a coincidence.

Cheryl considered sharing the information with Detective James but hesitated. If Detective James knew her father had been involved in the case, she might pull Cheryl from the investigation, citing a conflict of interest. And Cheryl wasn't ready to walk away. Since her father had a different last name, it would be easy enough to keep their connection a secret for now.

She continued reading. The report stated that Detective Don Travis' last known location had been Laketown University, where he had spoken with students and professors in the biology building. Three of the missing girls had been seen there before their disappearance. No one had any solid leads, but one student had caught Travis' attention—Wendell Washington. A brilliant but reclusive young man, Wendell had been a close friend of Evelyn Bridges and had shared classes with two other victims from the Divine Daughters sorority.

Despite Travis' suspicions, Wendell's alibi had checked out, and he had been ruled out as a suspect.

Cheryl closed the trunk, clutching the newly uncovered files, and walked into the station through the side door.

"There she is," Detective James said, spotting her. "I thought you might have gotten lost out there in this big ole town."

"Sorry, I didn't realize I'd be missed. I just had some things to review regarding the case. Can we talk?" Cheryl motioned for a private word.

"Of course. But first, let me show you what the team has uncovered."

"I'm listening."

Detective James led her to a table where she laid out the latest findings. "Those footprints we found in the woods? They belonged to the killer. They lead south toward the road. The shoes were Timberlands, size thirteen, confirmed by a deep imprint in the mud. Also, the victim was cut with a different knife than in the previous murder. And, just like before, we couldn't find a single drop of blood at the scene."

Detective James leaned back. "Now, what did you want to tell me?"

Cheryl hesitated for only a second before responding. "Detective James, I grew up in Laketown. On my way here, I was thinking about an old cold case—one from twenty years ago. There are some major similarities between that case and the recent killings."

Detective James perked up, intrigued. She shut the office door and took a seat, her full attention now on Cheryl. Unlike other officers Cheryl had worked with, Detective James had a certain presence about her—firm but empathetic. Cheryl sensed that she genuinely cared.

"So, tell me about this case. The Divine Daughters—is that the all-Black sorority?"

"Yes, that's the one. You've heard of them?"

"Of course," Detective James nodded. "My mother and aunts used to talk about them. That sorority is powerful, and those women don't play when it comes to their people."

Cheryl exhaled. "Well, that year was a devastating one for our town. The chosen daughters were murdered, and to this day, the killer was never found."

Detective James furrowed her brow. "Wasn't it believed to be the work of a serial killer?"

"That was one theory. Others thought it was a targeted attack. But no one really knows. What I do know is that the killings bear a striking resemblance to these new ones." Cheryl pulled out files from her black tote bag, laying them open for Detective James to see.

Detective James studied the documents. "So, each daughter was killed by a slit throat. Both wrists were cut—twice—forming a cross up to the mid-forearm." Her face darkened. "What kind of demonic shit is this? And the bodies were completely drained of blood? There wasn't any found at the scenes?"

"Exactly," Cheryl confirmed. "Not a single drop."

Detective James tapped her fingers against the table. "If all these cases happened in Virginia, we might need to take a deeper look at your hometown. I have a feeling that reopening this cold case could give us something useful."

Cheryl nodded. "I agree. I can also talk to people who were around at the time, see if I can uncover anything new."

Detective James leaned forward. "Listen, Woods. Tomorrow, I'm going to focus on speaking with Dr. Gaines' wife. But I want you to go back to Laketown and start digging into this killer's past."

"Understood. I'll leave first thing in the morning. I should get there around lunchtime."

Detective James stood and extended a hand. "Good. Keep me updated."

Cheryl shook her hand. "Thanks, Detective."

"Don't thank me yet," Detective James said with a smirk. "Just bring me something we can use. Good luck."

As Cheryl parked her Tahoe in the lot of the McDillion police station, she thought she heard something shift in her trunk. It was packed with various items—old boxes from home, a suitcase full of clothes, personal belongings, and materials related to her case. When she opened the trunk, one of the bags tumbled out. As she picked up the fallen items, she noticed something she didn't remember packing: an old box labeled with her father's name and his last case—D. Travis/Diviner Case.

Her eyes moved side to side in deep reflection. She was certain she hadn't put that box there. Then, a quick smile appeared on her face as she recalled her mother helping her pack before she left. Her mama must have slipped it in among the other boxes and bags. There was no other explanation. Still, it was her dad's box, and she had thought she had seen all of them—or so she believed.

Cheryl glanced around the parking lot. The bright lights illuminated the area, but there was no one near her truck. She only saw other officers entering the side doors of the building. From the looks of it, they were the team from the second killing, bringing in evidence for Detective James. She hesitated for a second, debating whether to wait and look through the mysterious box later. But something inside her urged her on. She needed to see what was inside. She grabbed the box and pulled it closer. As she stood at the trunk's edge, the bottom of the box suddenly gave out, sending its contents spilling onto the ground.

"What the—?" she muttered in frustration.

It must have been old and rotted. As she gathered the papers and photos, her breath caught in her throat. There, staring back at her, were pictures of her father, Donald Travis. His lifeless body lay in the woods, throat slit, his skin pale gray—drained of all his blood. Cheryl froze. She had always known her father had been murdered, but she had never known exactly how. Her mother had never spoken about it.

It had been over twenty years since she and her mother, Mary, had lost him. Yet, the pain still felt raw, as if it had happened yesterday. She flipped through more of the paperwork, uncovering pictures of the young women from her father's last case—the Divine Daughters. The images showed the victims with their throats cut, wrists slit in the shape of crosses, their bodies completely drained of blood. The reports stated that their remains had been found deep in the woods outside the Old Laketown community.

This couldn't be a coincidence.

Cheryl considered sharing the information with Detective James but hesitated. If Detective James knew her father had been involved in the case, she might pull Cheryl from the investigation, citing a conflict of interest. And Cheryl wasn't ready to walk away. Since her father had a different last name, it would be easy enough to keep their connection a secret for now.

She continued reading. The report stated that Detective Don Travis' last known location had been Laketown University, where he had spoken with students and professors in the biology building. Three of the missing girls had been seen there before their disappearance. No one had any solid leads, but one student had caught Travis' attention—Wendell Washington. A brilliant but reclusive young man, Wendell had been a close friend of Evelyn Bridges and had shared classes with two other victims from the Divine Daughters sorority.

Despite Travis' suspicions, Wendell's alibi had checked out, and he had been ruled out as a suspect.

Cheryl closed the trunk, clutching the newly uncovered files, and walked into the station through the side door.

"There she is," Detective James said, spotting her. "I thought you might have gotten lost out there in this big ole town."

"Sorry, I didn't realize I'd be missed. I just had some things to review regarding the case. Can we talk?" Cheryl motioned for a private word.

"Of course. But first, let me show you what the team has uncovered."

"I'm listening."

Detective James led her to a table where she laid out the latest findings. "Those footprints we found in the woods? They belonged to the killer. They lead south toward the road. The shoes were Timberlands, size thirteen, confirmed by a deep imprint in the mud. Also, the victim was cut with a different knife than in the previous murder. And, just like before, we couldn't find a single drop of blood at the scene."

Detective James leaned back. "Now, what did you want to tell me?"

Cheryl hesitated for only a second before responding. "Detective James, I grew up in Laketown. On my way here, I was thinking about an old cold case—one from twenty years ago. There are some major similarities between that case and the recent killings."

Detective James perked up, intrigued. She shut the office door and took a seat, her full attention now on Cheryl. Unlike other officers Cheryl had worked with, Detective James had a certain presence about her—firm but empathetic. Cheryl sensed that she genuinely cared.

"So, tell me about this case. The Divine Daughters—is that the all-Black sorority?"

"Yes, that's the one. You've heard of them?"

"Of course," Detective James nodded. "My mother and aunts used to talk about them. That sorority is powerful, and those women don't play when it comes to their people."

Cheryl exhaled. "Well, that year was a devastating one for our town. The chosen daughters were murdered, and to this day, the killer was never found."

Detective James furrowed her brow. "Wasn't it believed to be the work of a serial killer?"

"That was one theory. Others thought it was a targeted attack. But no one really knows. What I do know is that the killings bear a striking resemblance to these new ones." Cheryl pulled out files from her black tote bag, laying them open for Detective James to see.

Detective James studied the documents. "So, each daughter was killed by a slit throat. Both wrists were cut—twice—forming a cross up to the mid-forearm." Her face darkened. "What kind of demonic shit is this? And the bodies were completely drained of blood? There wasn't any found at the scenes?"

"Exactly," Cheryl confirmed. "Not a single drop."

Detective James tapped her fingers against the table. "If all these cases happened in Virginia, we might need to take a deeper look at your hometown. I have a feeling that reopening this cold case could give us something useful."

Cheryl nodded. "I agree. I can also talk to people who were around at the time, see if I can uncover anything new."

Detective James leaned forward. "Listen, Woods. Tomorrow, I'm going to focus on speaking with Dr. Gaines' wife. But I want you to go back to Laketown and start digging into this killer's past."

"Understood. I'll leave first thing in the morning. I should get there around lunchtime."

Detective James stood and extended a hand. "Good. Keep me updated."

Cheryl shook her hand. "Thanks, Detective."

"Don't thank me yet," Detective James said with a smirk. "Just bring me something we can use. Good luck."

The Bridges Mansion

A tall, slender, mature gentleman stood behind Grandma Violet, his posture militant yet composed as he waited patiently for his turn to greet me. His kind eyes sparkled when he smiled, exuding both strength and warmth.

"Ebony, this is Mason Bedford. He is the family's right hand. Nothing gets past him. He truly is the rock of the Bridges family empire."

"Great Mother, you are too kind. I am but a humble servant of a great house, and for that, I am grateful. Welcome, young Ebony Bridges. We have been expecting you and have waited a long time for this great family reunion," he said softly in my ear.

"Thank you so much for the warm welcome, Mister Bedford."

"No, please call me Mason. I'd prefer it."

"Of course, thank you, Mason. I have quite a few bags and belongings in the truck. It might take me a while to remove everything."

"Miss Ebony, you are a Bridges. You don't have to worry about retrieving any bags or belongings. I'll take care of it. You just go inside with your aunt and grandmother."

Entering the Bridges mansion felt like stepping into a sacred place, almost like a sanctuary. The grandeur was unmatched. High ceilings, rich wood paneling, and golden chandeliers adorned with natural crystals sparkled in the light. Mysterious symbols and ancient artifacts were subtly woven into the decor.

As I stood in the foyer, taking in its splendor, a tingling sensation crept over me. My hands and feet tingled first, the feeling spreading up both arms and down my legs. The hairs on my body stood on end, and my heart pounded like a bass drum in my chest. The air itself felt charged, as if the walls of the mansion were alive with energy.

Trying to steady myself, I glanced around to see if anyone else noticed, but all eyes were on me. My grandmother stood nearby, watching, studying my movements, hesitant to intervene.

"Ebony, are you okay? You seem a little woozy. Do you need some water?"

"No, I'm fine. I just felt a rush of something, and it kind of took my breath away."

"Well, we don't want that now, do we? Why don't you have a seat? I'll have Mason bring you a glass of water."

"Grandmother, your home is the most beautiful place I've ever seen. I am so thankful for your kindness. You didn't have to open your home to me."

"Oh, nonsense, granddaughter. This is your home now. You are welcome here. I know it has been a long day. Why don't you get showered and settled? We have so much to discuss, and I'm eager to talk to you about everything."

"I know, Grandmother. I'm looking forward to getting to know you as well. I have a lot of questions for you and Aunt Cassandra, too."

"Mason, please take my granddaughter to her suite on the third floor and ensure she has everything she needs to be comfortable."

"Of course, madam. Young Ebony, please follow me."

"Thank you, Grandmother. And thank you, Aunt Cassandra, for the safe and amazing drive."

"You are so welcome, niece."

This old mansion seemed endless. The foyer alone branched off in five different directions. Once you stepped through the grand double doors, there were countless choices of where to go. Since I was new here, I made sure to stay close to Mason so I wouldn't get lost.

To the left, a den blended into a formal seating area, complete with a full library, elegant Victorian-style chairs, and a grand piano positioned in the back. Family portraits adorned the walls, and glass cases displayed old, significant artifacts. The room exuded the essence of a Black history museum. Straight ahead, two grand staircases curled up the walls in a sweeping arc, framing a golden chandelier that hung above a wide hallway leading deeper into the home. To the right, a mirrored den housed another collection of artifacts, leading into an impressive home office or study. Every room radiated Victorian elegance and purpose, each one complementing the other. The Great Mother's crest appeared frequently, subtly embedded in the decor, even within the gold trim on the mansion's exterior. There was no doubt—this home was magical.

Following behind Mason, I couldn't help but notice how good he smelled. His cologne was strong but pleasant, blending seamlessly with the rich aroma of the house itself. It was as if he belonged to it.

"Okay, Miss Ebony, here is your room. We prepared everything for you, but if you need anything else, please let me know. I will do my very best to accommodate you."

"This is a room? This is my room?"

"Absolutely. Welcome home."

This wasn't just a room; it was an entire suite. An apartment, really. The queen-sized canopy bed stood high off the ground, its black frame draped in deep purple and dark violet bedding, adorned with eight to ten decorative plush pillows. Dark purple drapes framed the back windows, which overlooked a lush garden nestled within the sprawling backyard. A seating area with two comfortable chairs and a loveseat sat atop a luxurious dark purple and gold Persian rug in front of an already-lit wooden fireplace, its frame constructed of dark purple and black stones.

To the left of the bed was a walk-in closet, complete with a human-sized mirror encased in an ornate, thick black frame. To the right, the bathroom featured a black standalone tub with gold clawfoot details and matching faucet accessories, along with a glass shower lined with black marble.

My bags were already neatly placed, and the walk-in closet was stocked with hangers ready for my garments. After Mason's tour of my suite—which he informed me was the proper term for my space—I sank into the plush pillows of my bed, letting the exhaustion of the day settle over me.

Tears welled in my eyes as I reflected on everything that had happened. I had found my family, a legacy, and a home I never knew existed. But sadness crept in, knowing I couldn't share this moment with my mother. Why had she kept this from me? Had she been trying to protect me? Or was she trying to keep me from my own destiny? Compared to this, we had lived in near poverty. If she had come from this wealth and power, why had she been content giving me scraps of her world?

I needed answers. But for now, exhaustion won over curiosity. I let sleep claim me, knowing that tomorrow would bring more revelations.

Cassy

After an hour had passed since their arrival, Cassandra came down the stairs with a smile and found her mother, Violet, in the study. She was happy to be home and eager to talk to her mother about her new granddaughter. As she entered the room, Violet sat on a Victorian-style loveseat facing the door, her legs crossed as she flipped through an old book.

"Hey Ma, whatcha reading?"

"Hey honey, oh, just an old journal that I thought was lost to me. Now that I have it back, I can finally put it in its rightful place."

"What are you talking about?" Cassandra asked as she slowly sat down beside Violet on the couch. The room was warm and cozy, illuminated by the fireplace, soft lights, and a few candles.

"The Divine Daughters' sacred journal. Do you know that Mason found it in Ebony's things? He told me that as he was bringing her bags in, he could feel its power radiating from her suitcase. When he set it down, the book practically jumped out at him."

"Well, she actually told me she had the book and how she got it."

"Really? And how was that?"

"Evelyn, Mom. Ebony found it buried among her things after she was killed. She had set it aside as an eighteenth birthday gift for Ebony."

Violet's expression darkened with disappointment. She had long harbored frustration with Evelyn's life choices, and though she tried to contain her emotions, Cassandra knew her mother was a ticking time bomb, always on the verge of an explosion.

"From the day that child was born, she gave me problems. Your grandmother told me when she was delivered that this child, the middle child, would bring me pain. But I had no idea she meant this much pain."

Violet rose from the couch and stood before the fireplace, staring into the flames as memories flooded back.

"I tried my damnedest to be the best mother to the three of you—to protect you and keep you safe. But Evelyn... she had to have it her way. She never wanted to listen. She hated taking instruction from anyone, including me. Eventually, I just let her run herself right off the road because I was angry with her rebellious nature."

"I thought everything was fine. I mean, I knew we weren't perfect, but what family is? I had no idea Evelyn was so unhappy that she couldn't even come to me for help."

"Oh honey, don't feel bad. Evelyn was self-centered. She never wanted your help. She was always intimidated by you and the favor she believed you had with the family."

"Jealousy, Mother? Is that what you're saying? That my little sister was jealous of me?"

"Absolutely. From the moment she could walk and talk. She didn't know what to do about the darkness that resided within her. She placed herself in that mental space from the time she was five years old."

Violet's tone turned firm. "Evelyn had a powerful mind, meant to empower Maryan and this family's influence. But she had other plans."

"But why, Ma? Why did she leave us the way she did? I know that, as the Great Mother, you understand the truth of why things happen. Please, just tell me."

Violet inhaled deeply, preparing to be fully transparent with her eldest daughter.

"The ritual."

"What do you mean?" Cassandra asked, desperate for clarity.

"Evelyn learned about the great ritual of Maryan, the daughter of Sheiton. She was informed of our sacred practices and her role as the chosen one—the sacrifice to the dark lord, Sheiton. This ritual was meant to strengthen our family's power and improve the lives of all its members."

Cassandra's eyes widened. "What?"

"Yes, Cassandra. The reason you lost your twin baby girls was because your little sister refused to complete the ritual. When she ran away and wasn't found in time, the curse came upon us. Our family has been slowly dying ever since."

"Mother, this can't be. I know why I lost my babies—it was at the hands of an abuser, not some curse."

"I'm sorry, but it's true. As the Great Mother, it is my duty to bear the family's pain and protect us in every way possible. But because of the killings twenty years ago—our daughters, taken by an unknown enemy who managed to evade us while weakening us at the same time—we have endured silent torture within our own community."

Cassandra took a deep breath, trying to process everything. "So what are your plans now that we have Ebony?"

Violet's eyes gleamed with certainty. "I've already started preparing her for the sacred ritual. Her body is being cleansed. The moment she stepped into this home, the process began. The herbs were in the air, and I saw her body reacting. Her blood will be ready by Sunday."

Cassandra stiffened. "Mother, what are you saying?"

"Mason is watching over her. He has anointed her bed with essential oils and herbs, ensuring she inhales them and absorbs them through her skin. This will quicken the purification process."

Cassandra's voice softened with hesitation. "Ma, I feel bad for her. She's innocent. She has no idea what she walked into. Are you sure this is the only way?"

Violet's expression hardened. "It has always been our way, Cassy. This is the only way to find favor with our savior. He has set her aside for this moment, and we must take it."

The Blood Ritual

Late that night, Cain worked tirelessly in his ritual chamber, preparing for the first night of the Blood Harvest Moon. For the first time in over a century, the blood moon would remain in full bloom for three nights. With this power, Cain positioned himself at the forefront of Wendell's spirit, ensuring he would be present to perform and complete the all-powerful blood ritual.

The underground ritual chamber flickered with dim light from black candles arranged in an intricate circular pattern, their flames dancing alongside the curling tendrils of burning incense. In the center of the sanctuary, a large golden pentagram was traced onto the floor with white chalk. At its heart lay the obsidian altar, upon which Evelyn Bridges' lifeless body was carefully placed. The Mark of Malphas was written in Cain's own blood, accented with other demonic runes, preparing her as the ultimate offering. As the clock struck twelve, the blood ritual to commune with Malphas, Prince of Hell, began.

Cain stood before the altar, stripped to the waist, his upper body streaked with blood from self-inflicted cuts, the crimson liquid trickling down his chest in sacrifice. In his trembling hand, he held a ceremonial dagger, forged from obsidian—the Devil's Stone—and inscribed with infernal glyphs that gleamed under the dim light. His face, contorted in a mix of desperation and resolve, moved with fervor as he chanted incantations in an ancient, forbidden tongue, his bloodstained lips calling to the darkness.

With ritual precision, he mixed Evelyn's congealing blood with his own in a silver chalice, lifting it high above the altar. His voice rose, carrying his plea through the chamber, summoning Malphas—the cunning and treacherous Prince of Hell, son of Sheiton, the Dark Lord. The wind howled through the chamber, causing the candles to flicker violently, casting grotesque shadows over Evelyn's body. Cain's voice reached a crescendo as he invoked the prince's many titles:

"Prince of Treachery, Young King of the Damned, Son of the Morning Star, Master of Rebirth, Son of Our Savior, I summon thee!"

The room grew unbearably cold as his chant reached its climax. The sigil on the floor ignited with a hellish red flame, burning without consuming. A column of black smoke rose from the center, twisting and coiling like a living serpent. From the smoke, Malphas manifested—a towering, raven-like figure with the muscular form of a man, his black feathers shimmering with an eerie, oil-slick sheen. His piercing, glowing eyes locked onto Cain, radiating malice and curiosity.

A deep, echoing voice reverberated through the chamber.

"You summon me, believer, with blood and betrayal. Speak your terms, and be prepared to pay the price."

Cain stepped forward, blood still dripping from his wounds, his voice steady despite the tremor in his limbs.

"Prince of Hell, I, your humble servant, offer you this body and blood of Evelyn Bridges, daughter of the Great Mother witch of Maryan, Princess of Hell, and my own soul if need be. I ask you to bring her back, to place her dark spirit within her body so she may walk this earth again."

He paused, his voice hardening with rage.

"And grant me the power to destroy her family and all the great houses of this land. Their blood is their power—curse it. Poison it. Let their strength become their undoing."

Malphas tilted his head, a grotesque smile forming on his beak-like visage. He reached down, touching the body and the blood.

"A mother's love and a son's wrath—such potent fuel for damnation." He stepped closer, towering over Cain, his presence suffocating. "I will grant your wish. But know this: when mortals meddle with life and death, the consequences are rarely what they desire."

Cain's breath hitched. "I understand, Dark Lord."

"Do you?" Malphas asked with an amused glint in his eyes. "Then seal the bargain—carve my sigil into her chest with the dagger, binding her body as the vessel."

Cain's hand trembled as he knelt over Evelyn's corpse. He could feel Wendell's consciousness struggling against him, yearning to resist, but Cain's determination pushed him forward. As the blade cut into her flesh, the room erupted with hellish screams.

The sigil burned itself into Evelyn's skin, glowing a fiery red as her body convulsed violently. Black smoke poured from her mouth, eyes, and wounds, saturating the chamber. Her soul, tethered in limbo, writhed as Malphas's power forced itself into her vessel. Then, her eyes snapped open—but they were not her own. They glowed a deep, unnatural red, haunted by an otherworldly presence.

Malphas watched with satisfaction, his dark work complete.

"Maryan's daughter walks again," he croaked, his voice thick with mockery.

Then, he turned his burning gaze to Cain. "The curse you seek upon Maryan's servants will be your task. They must drink the liquid from the silver chalice before the end of the Blood Moon. Only then will their blood be poisoned."

Cain nodded solemnly, but Malphas's voice turned grave.

"Remember this, mortal: every gift I bestow carries a shadow."

With a final chilling laugh, Malphas vanished into the smoke, leaving Cain alone in the flickering candlelight with Evelyn's resurrected form. Her body breathed, her chest rising and falling, but her eyes remained closed.

The lingering scent of sulfur filled the air, marking the moment the world shifted—Evelyn Bridges had returned.

FAMILY BONDS

CHAPTER SIXTEEN
Family Bonds

Ebony's Nightmare Vision

The forest stretched endlessly into darkness, cloaked in a shroud of mist that swirled like restless spirits. Towering trees reached their skeletal branches toward the night sky, where a colossal moon loomed, casting an eerie silver glow onto the earth.

Ebony stood at the edge of the woods, her breath hitching in her chest as she spotted a lone figure moving through the shadows.

"Mama?" she called, her voice trembling, dissolving into the hush of the forest.

The figure didn't turn, didn't acknowledge her. Instead, it glided deeper into the trees, its presence both inviting and foreboding.

Something about it beckoned her forward, a pull she couldn't resist, though dread coiled in her stomach like a living thing. She hesitated, her bare feet sinking into the damp earth, but an unseen force urged her onward. Each step she took crunched on twigs and leaves, drawing her deeper into the labyrinth of darkness. The further she walked, the more the world behind her seemed to fade, until nothing remained but the forest and the shadow she chased.

Finally, she reached a clearing where the figure stood bathed in the moon's ghostly light. Ebony's breath caught as she saw the face she had longed to see—her mother, Evelyn. Familiar, yet somehow... wrong.

"Mama?" Ebony whispered, taking a cautious step forward, her hand outstretched.

Slowly, Evelyn turned.

Ebony froze.

Her mother's face was eerily flawless beneath the moonlight, her beauty untouched by time. But her eyes—they burned like deep red rubies, vivid and unnatural, filled with something ancient and malevolent. A wicked smile curled on her lips, sharp and knowing, exuding an energy that sent ice through Ebony's veins.

Ebony stumbled back, her pulse hammering. She wanted to speak, to scream, to run, but her body refused to move. Evelyn tilted her head, her expression unreadable, before lifting a hand and beckoning her forward.

"No," Ebony whispered, shaking her head violently.

The air thickened, heavy and suffocating, as if the forest itself was closing in on her.

Evelyn's form began to shift, her shadow twisting unnaturally, growing jagged and grotesque. The face that once belonged to her mother warped into something monstrous, something that should not exist. Those crimson eyes bore into her, stripping her bare, consuming her with terror so profound it felt as though her soul was unraveling.

A piercing scream ripped from Ebony's throat—

And then she woke.

Her body jerked upright, drenched in sweat, her hands trembling violently. The dim light of morning crept through the curtains, but it did little to banish the lingering dread. She could still feel the chill of the forest, the weight of her mother's stare pressing against her chest.

Was it just a dream? Or something more?

It had felt too real, too vivid, like she had truly been there. The forest. The figure. The warning.

Ebony pressed a hand to her racing heart, her mind spinning. If it wasn't just a nightmare, then what was it? And why did she have the awful feeling that her mother—or whatever had worn her mother's face—was waiting for her?

"Hello, Ma, I'm home," Cheryl called as she stepped through the front door.

Silence.

"Mama?" she called again, looking around the familiar walls of her childhood home. "You in here?"

A rustling sound from the backyard answered her.

A moment later, Mary Woods stepped inside, wiping dirt from her hands. "Cheryl, hey, baby! I didn't hear you. I was outside in the garden."

Cheryl's face lit up. "Oh, Ma, I missed you—come here, give me some hugs."

Mary chuckled, opening her arms. "You're a grown woman, but you'll always be my baby. Hugs and kisses, hugs and kisses." She pulled Cheryl into a tight embrace, squeezing her before planting a warm kiss on her forehead.

"Yep, and ain't nothing wrong with that." Cheryl grinned, stepping outside into her mother's sacred garden.

Lush, vibrant, and teeming with life, the garden was a world of its own. Herbs thrived in neat rows, their rich fragrances mingling in the air. This was more than just a hobby—Mary's garden was a sacred space, a source of healing. With the plants she cultivated, she created tonics, elixirs, and remedies for the family and community, using the gifts passed down through their bloodline.

Cheryl had witnessed her mother's power since she was a child. With a touch of the earth and whispered words in an ancient tongue, Mary could will plants to bloom before her eyes. But when Cheryl had grown older and refused to embrace the same gifts, her mother had stopped insisting, choosing instead to let her find her own path.

Now, standing here, Cheryl felt something stir within her.

"Mama, it's so beautiful and peaceful out here," she murmured. "I totally get why you spend so much time in this space."

Mary smiled, gazing over the garden. "Your grandmother used to sit right over there, petting her cat, Prissy. We'd spend hours working the soil together. She taught me everything I know. But more than that, she taught me the importance of staying connected—to the earth, to the ancestors, to the power that runs through us."

Cheryl hesitated. "Lately, I can't shake the feeling that something's pulling me back to that connection. Ever since I stepped into those woods last night… I don't know. It's like I want more, but I'm scared of what that means."

Mary turned to her, her expression knowing. "Mother Earth calls all her daughters, baby. She knows who you are, what you carry. She reached out to you in those woods for a reason. If she's drawing you in, there's something she wants you to see."

Cheryl swallowed hard. "Then how do I get her to show me the truth? To reveal who's behind these murders and why they're using her forest as a hunting ground?"

Mary studied her for a moment, then nodded. "Come with me. I have something that might help."

Cheryl followed her mother into the house, down the hall to a small room lined with dried herbs, glass bottles, and wooden boxes. Mary reached for a dark blue vial on the shelf.

"This is a potent tonic I made for a client, but I had some left over."

Cheryl took it, tilting the vial curiously. "It's blue. Does it taste good?"

Mary smirked. "Probably not. Most natural medicines don't. But this one contains three powerful herbs—mugwort, blue lotus, and holy basil."

"What do they do?"

"They'll put you into a conscious dream state. Make it easier for you to hear and commune with Mother Earth."

Cheryl nodded. "So… burn some sage and palo santo, drink this, and let her guide me?"

"Exactly."

Cheryl tightened her grip on the vial, determination settling in. "Okay. I'll do it."

Mary smiled, pleased. "Good."

Cheryl exhaled. "But first, I need to talk to you about something."

Mary arched a brow. "What is it?"

"Last night, I found an old black box in my truck. It had Daddy's name on it."

Mary's face stilled. "Oh?"

"I don't remember packing it, so I thought maybe you put it there."

Mary sighed, rubbing her temple. "I did. Your daddy left so much behind, Cheryl. I didn't know what to do with all those files. I just wanted to get rid of them."

"Why didn't you tell me?"

Mary hesitated, then waved her hand toward the garage. "Come on. I'll show you the rest."

Cheryl followed her mother into the garage, where an old storage room was hidden behind a stack of boxes. It smelled of dust and time.

"How many cases are in here?" Cheryl whispered, taking in the sight of dozens—maybe hundreds—of old files.

"Too many." Mary shook her head. "Your daddy was stubborn. He couldn't let go of any case, even when it wasn't his to solve."

Cheryl's fingers traced over a file marked *Washington 1960*. She pulled it free, flipping it open on the floor.

Mary sighed. "You got your daddy's look in your eye."

Cheryl smiled. "Yeah… I think I just found something."

Ebony sat on the edge of her bed, still trying to process the whirlwind of emotions from the past few days when her phone rang.

"Hello."

"Hey, Ebony, it's Cheryl. How's everything going with the Bridges?"

"Hey, Cheryl. Everything is good, actually. The family is so nice, and this old Victorian-style mansion is unbelievable."

"Yep, I told you your family had money. They've been one of the most powerful families in Laketown since it was established."

"Cheryl, I have never seen such wealth before, and with Black folks too—it's crazy."

"Yeah, I know. I grew up around them. Not everyone in Old Laketown is rich, but they own their houses and their land, and that makes them worth something. You know what I mean?"

"Absolutely."

"But listen, I was reaching out because I need to talk to you about a few things. You have a minute?"

"Yeah, what's going on?"

"Well, I'm actually back home in Old Laketown too."

"Oh really? When did you get back?"

"I drove in this morning because of the second killing."

"What? There's been another murder? Oh my god, what happened? When?"

"Yeah, Ebony, it's been all over the local news in McDillion. A man's body was found deep in the woods last night. He was killed the same way your mother was. We believe this might turn into a serial killer case."

"Oh my goodness. I feel so bad for his family. So does that mean this case might be connected to my mother's? Do y'all think it's the same person?"

"Absolutely, which is why I'm here. I've uncovered evidence of these same types of killings twenty years ago here in Laketown, and I believe the killer is from Old Laketown."

"What? How did you figure that out?"

"Ebony, did I ever tell you about my father, Detective Donald Travis?"

"No, you never mentioned your dad to me. Did he know my mother too?"

"Actually, he did. He was the detective on your mother's case twenty years ago when it was believed that she and four other Divine Daughters were killed. They were all murdered the same way—bodies found deep in the woods, drained of their blood."

Ebony gasped, gripping the phone tighter.

"I'm so sorry, Ebony, that was inconsiderate of me. Please forgive me. I haven't had much sleep—I've been working late nights trying to find this murderer."

"It's okay, Cheryl. I'm learning to deal with the harsh truths of life, day by day. But please, go on. I'm listening."

"Well, my father and his team worked tirelessly on those cases, and it tore him apart when he couldn't find the killer. Then one day, we got a knock on the door from the police... they told us he was found dead in the woods."

"Oh no, Cheryl. Are you serious? That explains your passion for what you do. You truly understand what it's like to lose a parent at the hands of a murderer."

"It's a pain that never really goes away. After that, I dedicated my life to finding his killer and helping other victims' families get the justice and closure they deserve."

Cheryl paused for a moment before continuing. "I found a large collection of files from these cases—my father's notes from twenty years ago. Before he died, he had a lead on a possible motive and a suspect—a man named Wendell Washington."

"Wendell Washington? I've never heard of that name before."

"After digging further, I found out that Wendell is the wealthy heir to Washington Builders and Landscaping, Inc."

"But Cheryl, why would he want to kill my mother?"

"I was looking through the old boxes of my dad's cases, and it turns out that back in the 1960s, Wendell's mother died by suicide just months after being hospitalized following a brutal attack by several men in town."

"Does it say who attacked her and how she was harmed?" Ebony asked, her curiosity growing.

"The medical report says she was raped, badly beaten, and left unconscious. She was in a coma for months. It also states that her five-year-old son, Wendell, was thrown against a brick wall and suffered severe cranial damage. He was found unconscious too but came out of his coma within a week."

"Did the police ever find the people who did that to them?"

"No. The case was never solved."

"So let me get this straight. You think your dad believed that this Wendell Washington guy might be the killer? That he's been doing all of this to get revenge or something?"

"Oh, listen to this—two years after the attack, at the age of seven, Wendell was diagnosed with dual personality disorder. His file states that he had a dark side he couldn't control, causing him to bully kids at school and even... harm small animals."

"Now that's definitely something to pay attention to. That's a huge red flag."

"Yeah, Ebony, I agree. That's pretty terrifying, especially at such an early age. They say serial killers start young. So what's next?"

"Ebony, are you going to the Blood Moon Festival later today?"

"Oh yeah, I wouldn't miss that for anything—not even my birthday."

"When's your birthday?"

"Today."

"What? Happy birthday, Ebony!"

"Thanks, Cheryl. It's nice to have a friend in town."

"Listen, let's meet up later at the festival, and maybe we can check out the Washington Estate while everyone is distracted."

"I don't know, Cheryl..."

"Excuse me, didn't you say you wanted to find out who killed your mother?"

"I did."

"We are this close to getting answers. You can't chicken out on me now."

Ebony sat there in silence, thinking about how much she needed answers—and how much Cheryl did too. What if this really was the man who killed both of their parents? They had to get to the bottom of this.

"Okay, let's do it. I don't have anything to lose anyway."

"Cool. It's a date. Go enjoy your birthday with your new family, and I'll see you later today for sure."

"Thanks, Cheryl. Talk to you later. Bye."

The last few weeks have been strange and life-changing in every possible way. I sit on the edge of my bed, taking in the grandeur of the suite, the elegance of the plush bedding, and the realization that I am in a Black-owned Victorian mansion, surrounded by a family I never knew existed. It's almost too much to process. The dream—or vision—still lingers in my mind, sending a chill down my spine. And now, after my conversation with Cheryl, I have learned that another person has been killed in the same horrific way as my mother.

Grief has overstayed its welcome in my life. I am desperate for something good, for something new.

Today is my birthday—my eighteenth birthday. Almost a grown-up, but I don't feel like it. Instead of excitement, I feel a strange awareness of the world, like I have stepped into something much bigger than myself. Birthdays always make me reflective. I remember my twelfth birthday, how I spent most of it in my room, lost in thought. Mama had baked a cake and tried to celebrate, but I refused to come out. Eventually, she called the Goodmans, and Charlotte came over for a sleepover to cheer me up.

Even back then, I felt a quiet distance between me and my mother. Of course, I loved her, but something about her never sat right with me. She never gave me straight answers about our family, about her life before I was born. And as I got older, those half-truths became more noticeable, more frustrating. Maybe, deep down, I always saw through the lies—I just hadn't known how to handle them.

Pulling myself out of my thoughts, I walk toward the bathroom and glance out the window. A beautiful setup is coming together in Grandma Violet's backyard. Two long tables stretch outward from the covered patio, draped in lavender and purple fabrics. Pink and purple roses and floral arrangements adorn every inch. I spot Mason, standing tall and authoritative, directing staff as they place in-ground metal light posts and hang decorations around the tables and patio.

I wonder what's going on, then I remember what Cheryl mentioned—the Blood Harvest Moon Festival is happening this weekend. Apparently, Old Laketown takes its traditions seriously, celebrating the changing seasons with elaborate gatherings.

After taking what feels like the best shower of my life, I wash and retwist my locs using the gel I packed. Stepping out, I notice something unexpected. A large bag has been placed on my bed, which someone has made while I was in the shower. That's a little creepy, but I push the thought aside. A card rests on my nightstand next to a stunning vase filled with pink and purple roses. I pick up the envelope and read:

Happy Eighteenth Birthday, Granddaughter.

I know you aren't used to big celebrations, so instead of surprising you, I decided to give you a heads-up. Please wear these traditional gowns and dress for the festivities downstairs. Later, we will begin the ancestral ceremony given to every chosen daughter of the Great Divine Women. Inside are two gowns—the purple one for your birthday and the red one for the ceremony. Matching shoes are in the boxes beside the bag. Come down when you're ready—everyone can't wait to meet you.

—Your Grandmother, Violet

I smile, relieved I took the time to retwist my locs. After moisturizing my skin, I add a touch of eyeliner, lashes, concealer, and a hint of blush. Then, I open the bag and gasp. The dresses inside are breathtaking.

The purple gown is a masterpiece—elegant and regal. The off-the-shoulder design frames my collarbone, and intricate floral embroidery cascades down the bodice and skirt in soft lavender hues. The Cinderella-style skirt is voluminous, designed to flow with my every movement. As I spin in front of the tall mirror, the fabric catches the air, making me look like I'm floating. I feel like Black royalty.

After slipping on the matching heels and spritzing on my mother's favorite perfume, I step toward the door, ready to walk into whatever awaits me.

As I emerge onto the second-floor landing, I take in the breathtaking view of the mansion. To my right, the grand stairwell spirals down in a circular motion, framing the foyer. To my left, a second foyer branches off into an East and West wing, each leading to three long hallways. Above me, a second set of stairs curls upward to the third floor, which holds two extensive hallways stretching deep into the mansion's upper level. Across from my suite, another grand bedroom mirrors my own.

The entire house has been decorated in honor of the occasion. Roses in deep purple, lavender, coral, and fuchsia adorn the staircases. Elegant streamers glitter under the lights, and in the center of the foyer stands a massive arrangement of roses on a round table.

I step toward the railing and gasp.

The mansion is filled with people.

Dressed in bright, formal attire, they move through the space like royalty at a grand ball. It looks like an Easter Sunday service, but grander. The moment I begin descending the staircase, a hush falls over the crowd.

Then, a familiar voice rings out.

"There she is, everyone—my granddaughter in the flesh. Happy Birthday, Ebony Bridges!"

A roar of cheers erupts through the house.

"Happy Birthday, Ebony!" the crowd chants.

My throat tightens with emotion. I have never experienced something like this before. Wiping away happy tears, all I can say is, "Thank you, everybody. Thank you so much."

"Aww, it's okay, honey. We're here for you." Aunt Cassandra appears by my side, pulling me into a warm embrace. Her hug is exactly what I need to steady myself.

"Auntie, you all didn't have to do this for me. I've never—
"

"It's okay, niece, we know. We wanted you to start your new journey by learning your true family's traditions. This is the Ancestral Birthday Brunch, a tradition for all direct descendants of the Great Mother's bloodline. Today is your day—not just to be celebrated, but to be welcomed into your family's legacy."

I swallow hard, overwhelmed by the weight of it all. "Oh, okay. Did you have one when you turned eighteen too?"

"Not quite," Cassandra says with a soft laugh, "but your mother did. Hers was even more extravagant than this one."

"I bet."

Before I can say more, a voice cuts through the chatter.

"So, this is my mysterious niece that everyone's been talking about."

I turn to see an older woman approaching—one of my many aunts, it seems.

"Yes, Aunt Mae, here is your niece, Ebony," Cassandra introduces.

"It's so nice to meet you," I say politely.

"Oh honey, you look just like Evelyn," Aunt Mae says, shaking her head in amazement. "I mean, she spit you out."

"Just a couple shades darker," another elegantly dressed woman chimes in.

"Indeed, Olivia," Mae adds. "I wonder where you got that chocolate complexion from, child."

"Oh, come on, Mae," says another woman, squeezing in between us. "You heard what happened—she has no idea who her daddy is, right, niece?" She gives me a knowing look.

I try to respond, but the conversation spirals into playful bickering between my aunts. Their personalities clash and intertwine like a well-rehearsed script. They remind me of a whirlwind—chaotic but full of love.

I smile, taking it all in.

For the first time in my life, I feel like I belong.

CHAPTER SEVENTEEN
THE RESURRECTION

CHAPTER SEVENTEEN
The Resurrection

The Old Laketown Clubhouse

I am in awe of the mystical beauty of Old Laketown. As we drive down the main road toward the clubhouse, the community is alive with an eerie yet enchanting energy under the glow of the Blood Moon Festival. A dense mist hovers above the red cobblestone street, weaving through the air like whispers of the past, casting an otherworldly presence over the town. From the beginning of the road all the way to the front porch of the Old Laketown Clubhouse—once the infamous *big house* over two hundred years ago—rows of vibrant red lanterns line the path. They sway gently in the cool night breeze, arranged in a deliberate pattern that adds to the night's air of mystery.

The street is crowded with festival attendees draped in black and deep-colored cloaks, concealing elegant gowns and finely tailored suits beneath their folds. The sight is almost surreal, as though this old community has been transported into another realm beneath the looming, blood-red moon, which hangs unnaturally large in the clouded sky.

Walking into the clubhouse, Aunt Cassandra and I are immediately met by Mason and his staff, who move gracefully through the crowd, carrying trays of hors d'oeuvres and serving the guests.

"My ladies, welcome. We've been expecting you," Mason greets us, though his gaze lingers on me.

"Well, thank you, Mason," Aunt Cassandra replies with a smirk. "But you know I had to make sure our guest was properly dressed and taken care of. And, you know, regal beauty takes time."

Mason nods approvingly. "Of course, Miss Cassandra. And if I may add, you did a spectacular job. Miss Ebony, you look magnificent this evening."

"Thank you so much, Mason," I say, trying not to blush. But truth be told, I feel absolutely stunning. My chocolate-brown skin radiates a warm glow under the festival lights, and my freshly washed and retwisted locs shimmer with natural brilliance. My crimson-red gown fits like a second skin, hugging my torso in all the right places, its intricate lace detailing tracing my neckline and long sleeves. The deep, flowing skirt cascades to the ground, billowing ever so slightly with my every step, adding an air of drama and grace.

Aunt Cassandra, like many of the women at the formal event, is draped in a black lace gown that clings to her curves with an undeniable allure. A black silk corset accentuates her figure, while her smooth, caramel-toned skin glistens under the flickering lanterns. Her gown is sophisticated yet striking, hugging her body with an effortless elegance that demands attention.

As we step deeper into the main hall, we are handed masks to complete our mysterious evening look. I find the perfect mask to match my gown and energy, while Aunt Cassandra selects hers with the same careful precision.

"Okay, it's time to mingle," she announces, adjusting her mask.

I hesitate.

"Come on, niece," she presses, nudging me playfully. "How are you supposed to meet any of Laketown's exceptional young men if you spend the entire evening sitting down?"

I stand, a little shy, unsure if I'm truly ready to "mingle." I never thought I'd be here to *meet someone*. Eighteen years old and I've never had a boyfriend. Mama never allowed it—said no one was ever good enough for me. Or at least, that's what she told me. But these days, I find myself questioning everything she ever said.

Before I can respond, a deep voice interjects.

"Well, well, somebody is looking fine tonight. It's the way that dress is hugging those curves for me."

I turn toward the voice, and Aunt Cassandra rolls her eyes playfully.

"Patrick, don't start," she says with a smirk. "You know I can turn it on when I *need* to turn it on."

"Yes, indeed, Miss Bridges," he replies, eyes gleaming with something unreadable.

"Ahem," Cassandra clears her throat, shifting the attention back to me. "Pat, let me introduce you to my niece, Ebony Bridges. Ebony, this is Patrick Maryland—the new dean of Laketown University and the head of the OLU Department, the most prestigious department at the university."

Patrick smiles, charming and confident. "Cassandra definitely knows how to make an introduction," he teases, winking at her before turning back to me. "It's a pleasure to meet you, Ebony Bridges. You seem to be the talk of the town—or should I say, the neighborhood."

"Really?" I ask, surprised. "I didn't know—"

"Well, word of mouth spreads like wildfire around these parts."

I return his smile and take a sip of my drink, engaging in the conversation. But then, something—or *someone*—catches my attention.

A young man strides through the crowd, and the moment our eyes meet, the world around me seems to pause. His sharp gaze softens slightly, but there is something powerful, almost *commanding*, in his presence.

"Auntie, who is that?" I whisper, trying to keep my composure while my breath catches in my throat.

She follows my gaze and arches an eyebrow. "Oh, that's Myles—the only son of the Holy Bishop of the Temple of God's Anointed. He's grown quite a bit over the last couple of years." She glances at me knowingly. "Why? Do you find him… interesting?"

I swallow hard. "I—I don't know. He just keeps staring at me. It feels like he's looking straight through my soul."

Aunt Cassandra lets out a full, belly-deep laugh, nearly spilling her wine. "Girl, you *are* dramatic. You *definitely* get that from your mother."

"But I'm serious, Auntie."

She smirks. "Well, if he's interested, he'll come over soon enough. Trust me."

Myles commands attention effortlessly as he moves through the moonlit festival. His deep mahogany complexion exudes a regal strength, his sharp yet warm features radiating confidence and quiet power. His hair, meticulously braided, is styled into intricate plaits that taper into a clean fade along the sides, adding to his polished appearance.

His attire is striking—a tailored black coat adorned with ornate golden embroidery that cascades across his broad shoulders and sleeves. The gold accents shimmer under the lantern lights, emphasizing his air of nobility. A silk golden cravat is neatly tied at his neck, complementing the embroidery, while polished brass buttons line his double-breasted coat with military precision. The golden designs on his cuffs suggest deep tradition and authority, making his entire look both commanding and refined.

Before I can say another word, a voice interrupts the moment.

"I see you've caught the attention of the son of the Holy Bishop," Grandma Violet states, appearing seemingly out of nowhere.

"Grandma—" I start, momentarily speechless.

Violet Bridges, the Great Mother, steps into the Blood Moon Festival with an aura that demands reverence. Her age-defying beauty radiates wisdom and power, making her presence unmistakable. Her caramel-toned skin glows under the soft lantern light, enhanced by a subtle golden shimmer.

Her hair—normally braided sleekly into a dignified ponytail—is loose tonight, cascading in soft, silken curls down her back. The effect is mesmerizing, framing her elegant features and emphasizing the high cheekbones, defined jawline, and almond-shaped eyes that hold the weight of generations.

She wears a gown fit for a queen. A deep, inky black fabric hugs her frame, shimmering with constellations of golden embroidery. The intricate patterns swirl across her bodice like celestial maps, pulsing faintly as though alive. The off-shoulder design reveals her regal collarbones, adorned with a choker of interwoven gold and obsidian beads. Sheer, embroidered sleeves extend to her wrists, ending in delicate golden cuffs.

The gown's skirt flows like liquid starlight, pooling around her feet in an ethereal golden glow. The hem is detailed with embroidery resembling flames and blooming flowers, flickering with life at every step. Tiny, glimmering crystals are scattered across the fabric, catching the moonlight like distant stars.

The air around her hums faintly with magic.

As she approaches, the festival seems to quiet.

All eyes are on the Great Mother.

The Great Mother

My grandmother, the Great Mother, Violet Bridges, is not merely attending the festival—she is its living embodiment. She and her sisters serve as a reminder to all who gather here of the ancestral legacy that binds the witches together, an unyielding force passed down through the bloodline.

"Oh, Mother, you look regal, like the great goddess that you are," Aunt Cassandra says, her voice filled with admiration and childlike fondness.

Violet smiles, radiating pride. "Thank you, daughter. And I must say, you did an exceptional job with this one." She and Cassandra both turn their gazes toward me, their expressions warm with approval.

"Thank you both so much," I say, feeling overwhelmed by their acceptance. "I truly feel like a princess. I can't tell you how happy I am to be here with you this evening."

Violet nods approvingly. "Well, you certainly made quite an impression on your aunties. They couldn't stop talking about you all day as we prepared for the evening."

I laugh softly. "They're hilarious. I'm really looking forward to getting to know each one of them. I love them already."

"And they love you, granddaughter. They love you dearly."

Aunt Cassandra suddenly straightens, her eyes lighting up with anticipation. "Oh, he's arrived," she says, her voice laced with excitement.

"Who?" I ask, following her gaze. But before she can answer, I feel it—the shift in the atmosphere.

As the Holy Bishop steps into the heart of the festivities, the crowd instinctively parts for him. Their lively chatter softens to murmurs of reverence. His movements are slow, deliberate—each step exuding authority, each glance commanding unwavering attention. His deep, resonant voice carries through the night air like a sacred hymn, igniting devotion among his followers.

Yet beneath the grandeur of his presence, I sense something else. A hidden ambition. A carefully concealed ruthlessness that makes his authority absolute.

The Holy Bishop is a force to behold. His almond-toned skin, lined with the wisdom of a man in his late forties or early fifties, glows faintly under the flickering festival lights. His salt-and-pepper beard and goatee are groomed to perfection, framing his noble, angular features. His sharp hazel eyes scan the crowd with quiet judgment, making even the boldest attendees lower their heads in respect.

His ceremonial attire is nothing short of magnificent—a seamless blend of gold and black. The deep golden fabric of his coat glistens as though kissed by divine light, tailored flawlessly to fit his broad shoulders and powerful build. Intricate black embroidery swirls like celestial symbols across the coat, weaving from the high collar to the asymmetrical hem that speaks of both tradition and calculated modernity.

Black trim accents his lapels, cuffs, and the epaulets on his shoulders, each adorned with delicate golden tassels that sway with his every movement. A crisp black cravat is knotted perfectly at his throat, complementing the black details on his sleeves and the ornate gloves he wears—both shimmering faintly, as if dusted with stardust. Gold chains drape subtly from his sides, connecting to finely wrought emblems of the Temple. His tailored black trousers lead into polished boots that complete the ensemble with an undeniable air of authority.

The festival air is thick with awe as he approaches my grandmother.

"Great Mother Violet Bridges," he intones, his voice smooth and deliberate. "You are a goddess in the flesh. It is always an honor to see you outside the Temple." He reaches for my grandmother's hands, his gaze lingering, filled with a reverence that makes the crowd murmur amongst themselves.

"The honor is mine, Holy Bishop," Violet replies, her voice calm yet commanding. "It is always a privilege to serve our savior and his church." She pauses, then gestures toward me. "Have you met my heir? My granddaughter, Ebony Bridges."

His brows lift ever so slightly. "Your heir? Well, I must prepare accordingly," he muses before turning his piercing gaze onto me. "Ah, Ebony Bridges. You must be the daughter of the late Evelyn. You are her spitting image."

I force a polite smile. "Hello, Holy Bishop. It is a pleasure to meet you, sir."

A hush falls over the crowd as they take in my presence, their whispers filling the space around me. It's clear that everyone here knows of my mother, though I'm sure few know the full truth. *Hell, I don't even know the whole truth.*

And because of that, I don't trust anyone in this town.

A sudden warmth spreads through my chest. A pulse. A flicker of something familiar and ancient. I feel a presence rise within me—*Onyx.*

She's getting stronger.

I fight to push her down, to keep control, but she refuses to be silenced.

"Please excuse me," I murmur, forcing a polite exit before I completely lose myself to her. I rush toward the restroom, barely making it into an empty stall before the fight is over.

Onyx storms to the forefront of my mind.

"Well, I see we've finally arrived," she coos, her voice a blend of amusement and menace. "Are you ready for our reunion?"

"Reunion?" I ask, my breath uneven. "What are you talking about? I'm just trying to enjoy the Blood Moon Festival."

"Oh yes," she purrs. "And after the festival comes the ancestral ritual. *That's* when we take our rightful place. When we become the most powerful being to ever walk this earth." She pauses, her tone darkening. "*This* is what Mama was trying to hide from us all along."

I stiffen. "No one has said anything to me about that."

"Of course not," Onyx sneers. "They're probably terrified you'll do what *she* did—run."

A cold realization slams into me. "Is that what the Bishop meant when he said he needed to *prepare?*"

"Exactly," she confirms. "He's the one who will conduct the ritual to unite us with the Dark Lord, Sheiton. But don't worry, dear Ebony…" her voice shifts, thick with satisfaction, "…we will be *so much more* than them. They won't be able to *contain* us."

She laughs then—low and wicked, the kind of laugh that chills me to my core.

I hate when she does that.

She terrifies me.

Or maybe…

I terrify myself.

If what she says is true, then everything I've been told is a lie. And I have no idea what happens next.

Cheryl entered the festival's main hall just as the Holy Bishop arrived, his presence commanding the attention of the entire room. The crowd around him was thick with reverence, but her eyes immediately sought out Ebony.

Draped in a striking crimson gown that flowed like liquid fire, Ebony looked breathtaking. But it wasn't just her appearance—there was something about her tonight, an air of power that seemed to radiate from within. Yet, it was the Great Mother who truly captivated the room. Her gown shimmered with an otherworldly glow, exuding a regal energy that set her apart from everyone else.

Cheryl was about to call out to Ebony when she noticed her sudden departure. Ebony moved swiftly, her posture rigid, her pace urgent. Without hesitation, Cheryl followed her into the dimly lit ladies' room.

The powder room was unlike any Cheryl had ever seen, exuding an aura of quiet enchantment. The Great Mother's emblem was etched into the walls, while blood moon lanterns cast an alluring, almost hypnotic glow. The air was thick with the scent of incense, a blend of herbs and something sweetly intoxicating. A single plush chair rested in the corner, accompanied by a grand mirror that reflected the flickering lantern light.

Cheryl instinctively scanned the space. It was empty—except for the last stall, where she could see the tips of Ebony's black and red open-toe heels peeking beneath the door.

She stepped forward, ready to speak, but then she heard it.

A voice.

But not just *any* voice.

A voice that sent an unnatural chill through her bones.

It was Ebony's voice, yet it wasn't.

The tone was unsettlingly low, like a whisper woven with something ancient and foreboding. The words slithered through the air, wrapping around Cheryl's mind like dark tendrils, each syllable dripping with malice.

Cheryl froze, her breath caught in her throat as she realized—Ebony was responding.

To herself.

But the reply wasn't in the same voice.

One moment, Ebony's voice was soft, uncertain, laced with innocence. Then, in an instant, it transformed—smooth, chilling, dripping with an eerie resonance that felt both seductive and predatory.

A dark harmony twisted between the two voices, a seamless blend of purity and corruption. Cheryl's heart pounded as a sharp, brittle laugh—like glass shattering in the dark—echoed from the stall.

Her instincts screamed at her to move.

Cheryl turned on her heel and rushed out of the bathroom, inhaling deeply as she tried to steady herself in the hallway.

She barely noticed when someone approached.

"Hey, are you okay?" Ebony's voice—her *real* voice—called out.

Cheryl looked up, forcing herself to regain composure. Ebony stood there, her expression warm and unsuspecting, completely unaware of what had just happened.

Cheryl hesitated before responding. "Wait… Ebony, hey! You look… amazing."

Ebony smiled. "Thank you! But Cheryl, what's wrong? You look like you've seen a ghost."

Cheryl swallowed hard, willing herself to focus. "Oh, I'm good. Just… feeling a little off. How's everything going? Are you having a good time?"

"Absolutely," Ebony beamed. "My grandmother just introduced me to the Holy Bishop. And," she smirked, lowering her voice, "I may have locked eyes with his gorgeous son, Myles."

Cheryl forced a laugh, trying to shake the uneasy feeling lingering in her gut. "I see you're getting around and mingling."

Ebony's eyes sparkled. "Oh, and Cheryl, I *love* your dress. Are you here alone tonight?"

"No, my mother was supposed to meet me. She's actually one of your grandmother's biggest suppliers—she handled the floral arrangements and herbs for the festival."

"Oh wow! That's amazing. I'll have to tell Grandma Violet that we're friends."

Cheryl nodded, then leaned in slightly. "Listen, did you bring your change of clothes?"

"Of course," Ebony said confidently. "I wouldn't miss this for the world. We're going to solve this case and stop these killings."

"Good. In an hour, we'll meet upstairs and change. My mother will keep an eye on our gowns."

Ebony gave a playful salute. "Sounds like a plan. So… you know exactly where we're going, right?"

"Oh yeah," Cheryl confirmed. "I even found a secret entrance to the property, in case there are cameras."

Ebony hesitated. "Wait. Are we… breaking into someone's house?"

Cheryl grinned. "Not exactly. Think of it as an *unscheduled investigation*."

Ebony sighed but nodded. "Okay. It's worth it."

Cheryl smirked. "It's worth *every* minute."

With their plan set, they went their separate ways. Cheryl slipped into the kitchen to check in with her mother while Ebony rejoined her family in the main hall.

As she approached the table, a deep, smooth voice stopped her in her tracks.

"Excuse me, it's Ebony, right?"

She turned and found herself face-to-face with Myles.

"Yes," she answered, tilting her head. "And you're Myles, correct?"

He smirked. "I see you've done your research."

Ebony returned his smirk. "I like to be prepared."

"Oh?" Myles raised a brow. "So you *knew* I'd come over and introduce myself?"

She laughed lightly. "Well, I *was* right, wasn't I?"

"Maybe so," he admitted. "But did you prepare for *this*?"

Before she could react, he took her by the hand and pulled her onto the dance floor.

Her crimson gown fanned around her as he spun her into an elegant waltz. The music swelled, and for a brief moment, the rest of the world faded away.

He led with effortless confidence, each step precise yet fluid. Ebony caught on quickly, but she couldn't ignore the eyes on them. People whispered, watching the way Myles commanded the floor with her.

She met his gaze, her pulse quickening. "You're a gifted dancer."

He smirked. "I try."

"So tell me, Myles," she teased. "Where are *you* from? I hear an accent."

His eyes darkened slightly. "Originally? South Africa. My parents adopted me when I was five and brought me here. Since then, I've been groomed to inherit my father's spiritual throne."

His words carried weight, but Ebony couldn't focus on them. Not fully. She was too lost in the way his presence felt—strong, controlled, magnetic.

For the first time since she'd arrived in Old Laketown, she felt something she hadn't expected.

Excitement.

Maybe Aunt Cassandra was right. Maybe it *was* time to spread her wings.

As the music faded, Myles walked her back to the table where her grandmother and aunties sat. He pulled out a chair for her, and she smiled as she sat down.

"A gentleman," Aunt Lili mused. "I like that."

"Honey, let me go find *me* one," Aunt Anita laughed.

"Oh, just *one*?" Aunt Olivia scoffed. "I need *two*, maybe *three*."

Ebony rolled her eyes, shaking her head with a chuckle. She turned back to Myles as he pulled a napkin from the table and wrote down his number.

"Call me once you get settled," he said smoothly. "Maybe we can hang out sometime."

Ebony took the napkin, her fingers brushing against his. "I'd like that."

"The pleasure was all mine, Ebony Bridges," he said before flashing one last smile and disappearing into the crowd.

Ebony exhaled, staring at the napkin in her hand.

For the first time that night, she wasn't thinking about murders.

Or secrets.

Or the looming ritual.

For now, she just let herself enjoy the moment.

Cheryl

As Cheryl walked away from Ebony, an unsettling feeling crept over her. She knew what she had heard in that bathroom, and for Ebony to come out acting like nothing had happened? Something wasn't right. There was more to this girl than met the eye, and Cheryl knew she had to keep a close watch on her.

Determined to clear her mind, Cheryl headed toward the back kitchen, where the real party was taking place. Laughter and the scent of home-cooked food filled the air as her mother, Mary, twirled around in a black dress, her white apron speckled with flour. The kitchen was alive with energy—old-school music blared from a nearby speaker, women sipped wine, and some danced while stirring pots and preparing food.

"Mama, how many glasses have you had tonight?" Cheryl teased, eyeing her with amusement.

Mary waved her off. "First of all, I'm grown. And second— hell, I don't know, maybe two or three."

"Mama."

"Uh-uh, Cheryl. Don't come in here with all that," Mary scolded, swaying her hips to the rhythm of the music. "This is a special celebration, child. The great mother earth is dancing with the great mother moon. Our gifts, our powers—they're igniting tonight."

She pulled Cheryl into the circle, and soon, they were laughing and dancing along with the other women. For a brief moment, Cheryl let herself enjoy it—until a thought struck her.

"Maybe that's why Ebony was acting so strange…" she murmured.

Mary slowed, her expression sharpening. "Ebony Bridges? That's the girl you've been talking about? The one tied to your case?"

Cheryl nodded. "Yeah. Have you seen her tonight?"

"No, but Violet's been talking about her plenty." Mary sighed, pulling off her apron. "You know I've been too busy making things pop around here. Let me see."

She stepped out of the kitchen and surveyed the festival crowd. Her gaze landed on Violet's table, where Ebony sat beside her grandmother and aunts.

Then, suddenly, Mary froze. A shudder rippled through her body, her breath catching in her throat. Without realizing it, she took a couple of steps back, pressing herself against the doorframe as if to shield herself from something unseen.

Cheryl frowned. "Mama? What's wrong? Are you okay?"

Mary barely heard her daughter's voice. For a split second—though it felt like an eternity—her mind was consumed by something she had witnessed earlier that day.

She had been upstairs in the private section of the clubhouse, preparing one of the rooms for the evening. The hall was quiet, filled only with the distant hum of activity downstairs. Then, out of nowhere, she heard it—screams.

Panicked, she had rushed toward the sound, thinking someone had hurt themselves. But before she reached the door, the screaming stopped. And then—she heard *him*. A voice so deep, so full of malevolent authority, it rooted her to the spot.

"Make sure they drink from this carafe and this carafe only throughout the night." His voice slithered through the air like a threat. "I'll be watching you. You know what will happen if you disobey me, don't you?"

A second voice—trembling, desperately—responded.

"Ye—yes, sir. Please don't harm me. I'll do exactly as you wish."

"Good boy. You'll receive payment when the job is done."

Mary's pulse pounded in her ears. The door in front of her flung open so violently she barely had time to react.

Paralyzed with fear, she did the only thing she could—dropped to the floor and pretended to be scrubbing it.

A shadow fell over her, and then *he* stepped into the hallway.

His skin was dark as midnight, his face partially obscured, but the high cheekbones, the sharp structure, and those deep, piercing brown eyes—she would never forget them.

Mary hadn't dared to breathe as he stared at her. And then, without a word, he walked past, his presence lingering like a cold imprint in the air. Now, standing in the festival hall, her eyes locked on Ebony, her breath grew shallow.

It was the same face.

"Mama, do you need to sit down?" Cheryl's voice finally cut through her daze. "I *told* you you had too much wine."

Mary blinked, forcing herself back to the present. "Oh, I'm sorry, honey. No, I'm fine. It's just been a long day."

Cheryl narrowed her eyes. "Are you sure? You looked like you saw a ghost."

Mary forced a tight smile. "I promise, I'm good." But inside, her mind raced.

If what she suspected was true, Ebony Bridges wasn't just some lost girl reconnecting with her roots. There was something more—something dangerous—hiding in her blood.

Cheryl exhaled, relieved. "Okay. Well, I'm leaving the festival early. Still working on my case."

Mary snapped out of her thoughts. "Where are you going?"

"I'll be changing upstairs," Cheryl said.

Mary's entire demeanor shifted. "*Don't* go past the second level."

Cheryl frowned. "Why?"

"Cheryl." Mary's tone hardened. "Did you hear me?"

Cheryl hesitated, then nodded. "Yeah, Ma. I heard you."

"Good." Mary exhaled. "Ebony's going with you, right?"

"Yeah, we planned to change in one of the private rooms on the second floor."

Mary pursed her lips. "Alright. But Cheryl… be *careful* with that Bridges girl."

Cheryl raised a brow. "What do you mean?"

Mary's voice lowered. "She got a funny look in her eyes. Kinda makes my blood boil a little."

Cheryl smirked. "You say that about everyone you don't trust."

"No, child," Mary muttered, her tone dead serious. "Not like this."

For the first time that night, a small chill ran up Cheryl's spine.

She nodded. "I promise—I'll watch her."

Mary exhaled and kissed her daughter's forehead. "That's all I ask."

As Cheryl turned to leave, her mother's warning echoed in her mind.

Something about this night wasn't right.

And whatever it was—she had a feeling Ebony Bridges was at the center of it.

CHAPTER EIGHTEEN
HER MOTHER'S LIES

CHAPTER EIGHTEEN
Her Mother's Lies

Evelyn

Evelyn awoke to the dim flicker of candlelight, the oppressive glow casting jagged shadows across the walls of the satanic chamber. She lay on an obsidian stone altar, the cold surface biting into her back. The scent of dried blood clung to the air, thick and metallic, coating her lips and face. She tried to move, but the weight of enchanted chains wrapped tightly around her limbs, leaving no room for escape.

She could feel him.

Even before she saw him, before he spoke, she could sense his presence lurking in the darkness, watching. He was near—he was always near.

Her voice came out hoarse but sharp. "First, you stalk me. Then, you kill me. And now, you bring me back—*like this*? Why are you so obsessed with me? What the hell do you want?"

A soft chuckle slithered through the room, laced with amusement and something far more sinister.

"I'm obsessed with you?" he mused, stepping closer. "Well, when you put it like that… maybe I am. But I have every reason to be."

She clenched her teeth. "Oh yeah? And what reason is that?"

His voice dipped lower, filled with venomous nostalgia. "You lied to me. You told me you loved me. You told me I was your one true love. And the crazy part? I *believed* you. I believed you would come back to me like you promised. But you didn't."

Evelyn scoffed. "Did you forget the part where they were *trying to kill me*? The same way they drained my cousins dry? Why the hell would I come back to your crazy ass?"

His laugh was slow, deliberate, and entirely devoid of warmth.

"You never loved me," he continued. "You loved *Walter*—the Holy Bishop. But you didn't love *me*. I *needed* you, Evelyn."

Her lips curled in disgust. "I *cared* for Walter, yes. But I cared for *you*, too. And trust me, the second he married that ugly wife of his, I wanted nothing to do with him."

He scoffed. "I was the one who helped you. *I* was the one who told you the truth about your family's history. *I* warned you about the sacrifice."

Evelyn's voice hardened. "And the day you *tried to kill me* was the day you lost everything. I will *never* forgive you for the hell you brought into my life. I've had to live a lie for too long and now my daughter—"

He cut her off with a sneer. "You mean *our* daughter?"

Her entire body tensed. "*Don't* you even *think* about touching my child. I will—"

"You'll do *nothing*." His voice turned cold as steel. "Elaine—or whatever your fake name is—*I* hold the power now. And you? You're going to do *exactly* what I say."

She pulled at the chains, rage igniting inside her. "I'm not doing a damn thing. And when I get my hands on you, Wendell—"

A cruel laugh echoed through the chamber.

"Wendell?" he taunted. "Oh no, I'm not that *weakling*."

He stepped forward, finally emerging from the shadows, his figure illuminated by the eerie glow of the candlelight.

Evelyn's breath caught in her throat.

The man before her was *not* the one she once knew.

His features were grotesque, twisted beyond recognition, his flesh marred with unholy markings. His once-human eyes now burned with an inhuman, fiery glow, filled with malice and something even darker—something that made her stomach turn.

"I'm Cain, *witch*," he spat. "And you're going to do exactly as I say. Because if you don't…"

His smirk widened, revealing sharp, unnatural teeth.

"Our little girl will be hanging from a long-leaf pine by midnight."

Terror gripped Evelyn's body.

Her chest burned, and though she couldn't touch it, she *felt* the Malphasanic sigil carved into her flesh—a binding mark, a permanent tether to him and the dark prince. She had no choice.

If she resisted, Ebony would die.

She turned her head, letting the silent tears streak down her face.

Her voice was barely above a whisper when she finally spoke.

"What would you have me do?"

Her tone was hollow, empty.

A surrender.

Cain grinned.

"Now *that's* more like it."

The Field Trip

After meeting Cheryl on the second floor and changing into more comfortable clothes, we snuck out without being seen. My mind was still replaying my dance with Myles, the way he held me, how effortlessly we moved together. Even my aunts were smitten with him.

"So, I saw you dancing the night away with Myles," Cheryl teased as she started the car. "He's really grown up over the years. Looks like he's gonna be as tall as the Bishop."

"Yeah, he really made my night," I admitted, smiling to myself. "Honestly, I can't stop thinking about him. Dancing with him in front of everyone was a magical experience."

"Aww, that's sweet, Ebony. He's a really good kid, too—very mature for his age."

"Yeah, and he has good energy. I like that."

The ride took us about twenty minutes, heading deeper into a rural area outside of the Old Laketown community. We were surrounded by thick forest as the road wound its way up the mountain. The air felt colder here, heavier. Cheryl slowed the car as we approached an entrance with a tall black iron gate. In the center of the gate was an intricate design of a tree, its branches sprawling like veins.

"That's nice," I said, admiring it. "Is that where we're going?"

"Yeah," Cheryl nodded, gripping the wheel. "But we're not going through the front gate. I found an opening along the property where the deer have made a path."

"The deer? So we *are* trespassing?" I sighed, shaking my head. "Oh my God, what in the world have I gotten myself into?"

"Look, Ebony," Cheryl said, glancing at me with a serious expression. "We're looking for answers. Two people have been murdered—and honestly, I think there might be *more* than that."

I stiffened. "What do you mean?"

Cheryl inhaled deeply. "After going through more of my father's old files… this was the last place he went before his death."

A cold shiver crawled up my spine. "Wait a minute, Cheryl. Are you telling me that there's a *possibility* your dad was killed here?"

"I don't know for sure," she admitted. "But I *do* know we need answers. And I think we'll find them here—at the Washingtons'."

A wave of unease settled in my stomach. What had I gotten myself into? I wasn't a private investigator like Cheryl. But looking over at her, I saw something in her eyes—a determination I couldn't ignore. She *needed* me to be here, too. Even though she was older than me, there was a youthful energy about her, an urgency, like she had been waiting for this moment her whole life.

And I wasn't about to let her go through it alone.

"Well," I sighed, forcing a small smile, "we've come this far. Let's keep going, *friend*."

Cheryl glanced at me, her lips curving into a small smile. "You know I got your back, right?"

"You better, *private eye Woods*."

We laughed quietly, then crept toward the wooden break in the fence, squeezing through one by one.

The Den

We walked for what felt like at least a mile through the deep woods. Cheryl used the GPS on her phone to guide us in the right direction. But when we arrived at the location, it wasn't a house at all. This was definitely somebody's mansion. It looked like a modern log cabin perched on a hill, massive and looming over the land. It was the biggest mountain cabin mansion I had ever seen.

"Damn, this place is huge. This house doesn't look anything like the Old Laketown mansions," I whispered.

"It looks like it has three levels too," Cheryl observed.

"Four, including the basement," she added, pointing to the rectangular basement windows.

I followed her gaze. "I bet you could squeeze through there."

She smirked. "We both could. You wanna start in the basement?"

"That's usually where the good stuff is hidden, in my experience."

Before Cheryl could respond, a deep mechanical hum filled the air. The garage door was opening.

We dropped low behind a thick patch of trees, hearts pounding. A large, blacked-out truck pulled out of the garage, its tinted windows making it impossible to see inside. We held our breath as the vehicle backed out, moving down the winding road. As it neared the tall iron gate, it opened automatically, allowing the truck to slip through before sealing shut again.

Cheryl exhaled. "Perfect timing. Let's go."

We moved quickly toward the house, but a sharp snap behind me made my entire body freeze. It wasn't a leaf crunch or a harmless twig—it was deliberate. Close.

"Wait," I whispered, my throat dry. "Did you hear that?"

Cheryl stiffened. "Yeah."

A chilling sensation prickled my skin, like something was watching us. I felt it. Heavy. Predatory.

I didn't dare turn around.

"Cheryl," I barely breathed, "something's here."

Slowly, she turned her head toward the treeline. The moment her eyes landed on whatever lurked there, her face drained of color.

"Oh my God," her voice trembled. "Ebony—there's something watching us."

"What is it?" I still couldn't bring myself to turn.

"Two red eyes," she whispered. "Up by the fence."

I swallowed hard. "Is it a dog?"

Cheryl hesitated. "I don't think so."

The sound of something shifting—low, heavy, primal—sent a jolt of terror through me.

"We have to get inside," Cheryl hissed. "Now. Run!"

I didn't wait for more convincing. We took off toward the house, running full speed. I could hear it moving behind us, the rhythmic pounding of massive paws against the ground. Too fast. Too close.

But then, just as we neared the house, the sound stopped.

Cheryl reached the basement window first, her hands trembling as she slid it open. "Get in!" she urged.

I didn't think. I dove through the opening, landing awkwardly in a metal sink. Cheryl followed a second later, pulling the window shut behind us.

For a moment, we just sat there, gasping for breath.

"I think it's gone," Cheryl whispered. "The back light from the house must've scared it away."

I groaned, clutching my chest. "I swear to God, I almost pissed my pants."

Cheryl let out a nervous laugh, shaking her head. "Me too."

We climbed out of the sink and took in our surroundings. The basement was not what I expected. Instead of storage boxes or old furniture, we stood inside a clinical-looking laboratory. Stainless steel cabinets lined the walls. Microscopes of different sizes were arranged on sleek countertops. In the center of the room sat a human-sized metallic bed, pristine and sterile.

And then, there was the refrigerator.

A huge glass double-door fridge, humming softly in the cold, sterile air.

Cheryl flicked on a light and approached it cautiously. Peering through the glass, her body tensed. "Ebony," she called, waving me over. "Come look at this."

I stepped closer, my stomach twisting.

Inside the fridge were rows of blood vials, each carefully labeled.

Cheryl pulled out her phone, snapping pictures, but then her breath hitched. Slowly, she reached inside and pulled out a vial.

The label read D. Travis.

Her hands shook. "Oh my God," she whispered. "This is it. I knew it. Wendell Washington killed my father."

She turned, eyes wild with emotion. "And these? These are all his victims."

I swallowed hard, scanning the other labels. My mother's name wasn't there.

"I don't see Evelyn's name," I muttered. "What do you think that means?"

Cheryl wiped at her face, her voice unsteady. "I don't know… but there has to be an explanation."

I reached out, touching her arm. "I'm so sorry, Cheryl."

She nodded, blinking rapidly. "It's fine. It happened years ago. But it still hurts."

I knew that pain all too well.

Cheryl took one last photo before carefully placing the vials back inside. Then, without another word, she turned and walked toward a dimly lit hallway.

The deeper we went, the stronger the scent became— blood, sulfur, burnt incense.

When we reached the end of the corridor, Cheryl flipped on a small wall lamp. A dull yellow light illuminated the room, casting eerie shadows over the walls.

We stood inside a sanctuary.

But not a holy one.

Black candles flickered in the corners. Symbols, sigils, demonic markings covered the walls, floor, and ceiling. The air throbbed with an unspoken presence, something ancient and watching.

I swallowed hard. "What kind of place is this?"

Cheryl's voice was tight. "A ritual den."

I scanned the room, my stomach turning at the sight of dried blood coating the floor. "This is where he does it, isn't it? The sacrifices."

Cheryl nodded grimly. "Yeah."

I didn't know what was worse—the fact that it happened here or the evidence that proved it.

As Cheryl took more pictures, something caught my eye—a small framed photo sitting atop a side table near a closed door.

I stepped closer. It was an old photograph. A young Evelyn. My mother, holding hands with a man who looked just like me. My breath caught. My hands trembled.

Cheryl appeared beside me, peering over my shoulder. Her face twisted into something sharp, dangerous.

"I knew it," she murmured, gripping the frame tightly. "I knew you were his child."

I flinched at her tone. "Cheryl—"

She turned to face me fully, anger burning behind her eyes. "You're his daughter, Ebony. Wendell Washington's. I just needed proof. And now I have it."

My heart plummeted. "Even if that's true, I don't know this man. I—I'm not him!"

The cold fury in her stare made my stomach churn. Before I could say another word, a voice shattered the tension.

"Hello?" A muffled sound came from the closed door. "Is someone there?"

Cheryl and I both spun toward the source.

A second voice, weak but desperate. "Please… help me! He'll be back soon!"

Cheryl's jaw clenched. "Who the hell is that?"

A cold dread settled over me. My pulse pounded. I knew that voice. My body moved before my brain could catch up. I ripped the heavy door open—and what I saw knocked the air from my lungs.

There, inside a cage, dressed in a blood-stained white gown, was my mother.

Evelyn. Alive. Chained like an animal.

My breath came out in a ragged gasp. "Mama?"

She lifted her head slowly. Her eyes—red, glowing, inhuman—locked onto mine. She smiled, lips cracked and dry.

"Ebony," she whispered. "I knew you would come."

"Ebony, my baby girl, I knew you would come. I knew you would come for me."

"How are you here? How are you alive right now?"

"He took me. He took my body."

"What do you mean, he took your body?" Cheryl demanded. "We saw the photos of you dead, then cremated. How is this possible?"

Evelyn's gaze flickered between us, her glowing red eyes narrowing. "Ebony, who is this—? Wait, Cheryl? Cheryl Woods, what the hell are you doing here with my daughter?"

I stepped closer, my breath shallow, my hands gripping the bars. My mother—if she was still my mother—looked nothing like the woman I remembered. Her once warm, caramel skin was now pale and drained of life. Dried blood clung to her tangled hair, and the air around her reeked of sulfur. My stomach twisted as my eyes traced the horrifying sight of the carved sigil burned into the center of her chest— the same symbol we had seen on the walls of the den.

My voice dropped, filled with both fear and revulsion. "Mama… what happened to you?"

She didn't answer.

The silence stretched, thick and suffocating.

Then, deep inside me, something stirred.

A familiar heat built in my core, rising steadily, demanding to be released. This time, I didn't fight it. I let it come.

Onyx was waking.

My neck jerked involuntarily, a sharp twitch. My body trembled as the energy flooded through me, stronger than before, more insistent. I gripped the bars tightly and all went silent.

"No more lies, Mother. Speak!"

Onyx's eyes glowed ruby red as she peered into my mother. Her face and body were Ebony's, but her demeanor was not. She was much more demanding and assertive. Her strength was like that of a young, fierce warrior but with dark goddess energy. She embodied dark feminine power, waiting patiently for her time.

Evelyn, facing the wall, slowly turned to face Onyx.

"Lies, huh? You have no idea what I've been through. Lies were necessary, daughter. I gave up everything for you. I lied to keep us both safe. I sacrificed my life, my family, and my dreams to protect you."

"You didn't have to do all of that. You should have gone to your family. They would have been there for you."

"Cheryl, what do you know about my family? Who are you to try to tell me about my crazy family?"

"I know that your mother—"

"My mother? You mean the woman who tried to kill me and sacrifice me to the damn devil? Or do you mean my aunts who were all in on it? Maybe you're talking about my messed-up older sister who thinks she's little miss perfect but would do anything for my mother's approval—even drink my blood."

Cheryl just stood there in awe, taken aback, unable to respond.

"This whole community is wicked as fuck, Cheryl, and you know it. Oh, don't you stand over there and act like you and your crazy mama ain't got that witchy shit too. Honey, I know all about you 'Woods Women.'"

"Don't start, Evelyn. Leave my mother out of this."

"Oh, I would if I could, but I can't, and there ain't nothing you can do about it, little Cheryl. How else do you think I was able to hide in the woods and escape? It was your mother and her sisters who gave me shelter when Walter and his father's men were after me."

"That's not true. You're lying. My mother would never get involved."

"Girl, you don't even know who your mama really is. Outside of the Diviner Women, the Woods Women are the most powerful coven in Old Laketown."

Cheryl looked at Evelyn, shocked and confused. She had never known that her mother was a witch; she just thought she had certain gifts and loved helping people.

"Yeah, see, you don't know because you decided you wanted to be a man and do man's work. You broke your mother's heart and broke tradition. Now you're out here with no power and no true understanding."

"I know my family history, and I know—"

"Oh, please. You don't know shit. Before you come in here trying to judge us, check your own self at the door, honey. Because with these blood eyes, I see all of you and everything you try to hide in your closet."

"Mama!" Onyx screamed. "Tell me what happened to you!"

"I'm what happened to her!"

Cain's voice boomed as he flung open the other side of the double closet door, an obsidian-handled knife gleaming in his hand. In one swift motion, he grabbed Cheryl and slit her throat.

"No!" Evelyn and Onyx screamed as Ebony's body collapsed to the floor.

"Ebony! Ebony! Wake up! No, don't you touch my baby!"

Cain dragged Cheryl's convulsing body back into the den, then lifted Ebony off the floor, shutting both doors behind him.

"Please, don't hurt my baby. I'll do whatever you want. Just don't hurt my baby girl," Evelyn sobbed, pleading for her daughter's life.

THE DEVIL

CHAPTER NINETEEN
The Devil

The Dream Connection

Tightly fitted chains around her ankles and wrists left deep scars and bruises. The chains were long enough to allow her to stand, lie down on the cold concrete floor, and even cross her legs if she sat close to the wall. The rectangular window placed at the top of the concrete wall provided a perfect view of the blood moon for a couple of hours each night. Sadness, fear, and anger pulsed through her veins. She hated feeling hopeless. She wasn't strong enough to break the chains or rescue herself from bondage, but one thing she could do was go within and seek a connection in the subconscious, just like she had before.

Under the moonlight, she sat in silence and used her spiritual power to connect with Ebony. She had no idea when Wendell would return or what he planned to do to her, but a part of her still believed that her daughter was alive and, by now, safe somewhere. Evelyn began to chant, and in time, her body lay propped up against the wall while her mind and spirit traveled to a different location.

In what looked like her old suite in her family home, she found her daughter, still dressed in the clothes she had worn earlier. In a dream state, she called her name.

"Ebony. Ebony, honey, wake up."

"Mama, is that you? Oh my God, where am I? How did I get back here?"

"Ebony, calm down. You're safe, I think. It looks like Wendell brought you back home. But for now, you're dreaming."

"This is a dream?"

"Yes, I'm not really here with you in my old bedroom. I'm reaching out to you again through your subconscious."

"So, the last dream I had of you in the woods was real?"

"Yes."

"I knew it. It felt so real. It's like I could feel everything. Ma, I'm so sorry for passing out on you like that. It's just something that's been happening to me more lately."

"What's been going on? I hate that I'm not there for you, honey."

"Ma, you're not here for me because of your bad decisions. I love you so much, but I can't explain how betrayed and angry I am. I didn't deserve this."

"Don't you think I know that? I'm ashamed of my own actions. I just thought that those same actions would allow us to live a better life—a life away from fear and manipulation from others."

"But it didn't. Now look at us. We are even worse off than before."

Mama's spirit glided across the floor, then stood in front of the fireplace. With a shameful look on her face, she turned back to me, sitting on the side of the bed.

"Ebony, after my eighteenth birthday, I received my ancestral gifts. That's when my mother and the family knew that I was next in line to become the Great Mother of Old Laketown. I went to Laketown University for college and majored in biology. I knew that I wanted to be a nurse and maybe even a doctor one day." With anger creeping into her eyes, she turned and faced the fire.

"But all that changed my junior year when I met Wendell Washington. He was also a biology major and absolutely gorgeous. We hit it off immediately. He was deeply involved in the church, so we would see each other in school and at church. We spent a lot of time together," she said, a slight smile forming at the corners of her mouth.

"The more time I spent with him off campus, the more I started to notice his true nature. Wendell had DID—dissociative identity disorder—real bad," she expressed, her eyes widening.

"He was violent towards animals and sometimes people, but he tried his best to hide it from me. One day I asked him about it. We sat down, and he told me about his condition. He said that he wasn't born with it, but it was brought on through a traumatic event that happened during his childhood. But by the end of the conversation, he was ranting and raving about getting revenge."

"So you still don't know what happened to him for sure?" I asked.

"Mama, is Wendell Washington my father?"

"Yes."

"Did he know about me being born? Did he know you were pregnant with me?"

"I wanted to tell him, but he is so evil. He tried to kill me. I couldn't risk it. He's been in denial, I guess. Wendell is a dark, selfish type of man. He wants you to believe the lies that come out of his mouth so you won't question his motives."

"Ebony, you have every right to be angry with me, but please know that I lied to you your whole life to hide you from the real truth of this world. I was young, and running away was the only way I felt I could control our life. I wanted better for you. To be honest, I wanted better for myself too.

"Wendell Washington was the worst father a child could ever have. He's a bully, a liar, and a manipulator. I'm so sorry for choosing such a horrible man to lay down with and conceive a child. It was the worst decision I ever made, and it has haunted me for over twenty years."

Tears fell from my eyes as I witnessed my mother finally being honest. It hurt me so much to see how heartbroken she had been over this man—my father, Wendell Washington. I had to make him pay dearly for the pain he caused my mother. I didn't care if he was my father. He would pay for this.

"Mama," I said, wiping away tears. "Why did he murder you and all of those people?"

"He is a devoted worshipper of the prince of hell, Malphas. He worships him through the dark sector of the church."

"So people who go to church believe in God and the devil?"

"Absolutely. Historically, in this town and some others, Black people—descendants of slavery—turned to the slave master's enemy, Sheiton, the Dark Lord of Hell, and his son, Malphas. Maryan, Malphas's wife, was the dark princess."

"I thought Black folks loved God?"

"They do, more so now, but for hundreds of years, the white man's God only helped him and his family. We were forced to worship a God who didn't care about the gruesome nature of what was happening to us every day and every night. My great-great-grandmother, Mary, had no choice. She did what she had to do for her family and her people."

"I see. I guess I never thought about this darkness—my dark nature—in that way. I'm not bad, but I'm not all good either. There's balance in me."

"You have both sides, and your daughter will be more powerful than all of Sheiton's spiritual offspring. Because you have Wendell's DID too."

I gasped, holding my breath in shame. "I'm sorry, I—"

"It's okay. It's always been inside of you. I noticed it when you were a child. You would play with her and talk to her a lot. But things took a dark turn once I was murdered by your father."

"It was so traumatic, I couldn't deal with the impact of it all. Then, all of a sudden, she started showing up in my dreams, my daydreams, and in my subconscious and conscious mind. Now she takes over and causes me to black out completely."

"Just like Wendell. Cain..."

"What?" I asked.

"Wendell's dark spirit is named Cain, after the first murderer of Sheiton. What's yours?" she asked with a curious look.

"Onyx. She represents the death of lies and weakness within me. I feel like she is my higher self—black and absolutely beautiful."

Mama's eyes shifted left and right frantically. "He's coming..."

"Who's coming? Mama, are you okay?"

"I have to go. Cain is coming for me. Ebony, know that I love you. Please forgive me for whatever I do from this point forward. I'm sorry. Ebony, I'm so sorry for everything..."

"Mama, don't go! I love you too! Mama, please, it's okay! I forgive you, Mama!"

I screamed as her body became engulfed in flames from her feet up to the top of her head. But she didn't scream. She just submitted to the flames and closed her eyes. Then she was gone.

I woke up in a panic. I looked around and saw that I was back in my room, lying on my bed. The fireplace was lit, but there was no sign of my mother anywhere. But no matter what, I knew that dream was real. The most realistic dream I had ever had in my life.

Cheryl's Gone

Tears fell as I thought of my mama and everything she had been through. I just couldn't imagine dealing with so much chaos. I sat up and reached for my phone to call Cheryl, but suddenly, my heart dropped.

Cheryl's gone!

Oh my God, what happened to Cheryl? Was she really dead? Did Cain or Wendell kill her?

I wanted to call her, but my hand started shaking so badly that I stopped. I couldn't deal with this right now. I had to be going crazy. I walked into the bathroom and stood in front of the mirror, reflecting on last night. Every instinct in me told me that Cheryl was dead for real. I kept seeing her throat being slit with a long, handheld knife with an obsidian handle.

A knock at the door startled me.

"Ebony, honey, can we come in?"

Aunt Cassandra and Grandma Violet entered, carrying a breakfast bagel, cream cheese, and a tall glass of orange juice.

"Hey, sweetie, how are you feeling? We wanted to check on you. We brought breakfast," Grandma said warmly.

"Thanks, Grandma. I'm doing okay," I replied, though I wasn't sure if I was telling the truth.

"You know, we looked for you last night at the festival. You didn't tell anyone that you left. We were worried sick."

"Thank God we found you asleep on the cot in the garden under the blood moon. Was it all too much for you? Maybe it was just too many people?" Aunt Cassandra asked.

"Yeah, it was a bit much. I didn't want to ruin y'all's night. Everyone was dressed so beautifully, and I didn't want to dampen the mood. Please forgive me for any stress I caused."

"Yes, well, all is forgiven now, honey. Eat up—tonight is the big night."

"What big night, Grandma Violet?"

"Have you forgotten about the ancestral ceremony?"

"Oh… but I don't know what to do."

"Well, first, you will wear this red gown and these black boots because the ceremony will be outside, not too far from the church grounds, along with this red velvet cloak. Don't worry—we will handle the rest."

"But Grandma, who is gonna be there? I'm really not in the mood to be around a lot of people right now."

"Oh no, don't you worry about crowds. This ceremony is only for the leaders in the community and the church. The Bishop, the Diviner Women, the Wood Women, the Mayor, and the heads of the other influential families. It's about twelve people—well, thirteen, including you. This is a very ancient event, and all family heads must be in attendance."

"Oh… okay."

"Don't worry, you'll be fine," Aunt Cassandra said in a reassuring manner.

Just then, the surprising sound of the doorbell ringing made Grandma Violet jump slightly.

"I wonder who that could be," she murmured.

Mason answered the front door in his usual militant manner. He retrieved what looked like my festival dress from someone's hands and spoke the name of Mary Woods as a visitor while walking toward the closet.

"Mary?" Grandma's voice held a note of shock as she came down the stairs.

The two women embraced, then headed to the study to talk in private. Aunt Cassandra and I followed at a distance, listening in for a moment before stepping away.

"Mary, come in. Please have a seat. What seems to be the matter?"

"Violet, I know this might sound crazy, but have you seen my daughter, Cheryl?"

"No, I saw her last night—maybe once at the festival— but that's it. Have you called her phone?"

"Oh yes, I've been calling her all night, but it goes straight to voicemail. I tried to shake it, but my gut—my intuition—is screaming that something bad has happened to my baby."

"Oh my goodness, Mary. No, she has to be okay, right? She was just with you last night. There's got to be a better explanation."

"What about your granddaughter? Has she seen Cheryl?"

"I don't know, but I can ask." Grandma turned her head toward the stairs.

"Ebony!" she called.

I stepped out of my room to answer. "Yes, Grandma?"

"Have you spoken to Cheryl Woods or seen her?"

"Not since last night. We hung out after the festival, and she brought me home. I actually tried to call her, but she didn't answer. Maybe it went to voicemail or something."

"Okay, honey. Her mother's here. She was worried about her."

"Oh, I'm sorry. I wish I could be of more help."

Grandma Violet looked at her friend and said, "Everything is going to be okay, Mary. Just be patient, and she will come around."

"I hope you're right," Mary said, her voice trembling. "Because the last time I felt like this was the night my husband was killed. Honestly, I don't think I can bury another family member."

Grandma Violet reached out and pulled her friend into a tight embrace. She would do everything she could to help find Cheryl.

The Flame

Wendell burst through the doors of the caged closet room where Evelyn sat behind the bars, chained to the floor with her back against the wall. The time had come for her to prepare for whatever Cain would command her to do. She knew she had no choice but to comply or face the unthinkable.

"Evelyn, wake up. It's time." He tossed a clean white gown and a black velvet cloak onto the floor in front of her.

"What is this? What do you want from me? What have you done with my daughter?"

"Calm down. Ebony is safe. I wouldn't harm her. I need her to carry out my plan."

"Plan? What plan?"

"The one where only one person can come back to stop these powerful murders."

"What are you talking about, Wendell?"

"I know you think that I'm… I mean, that Cain is evil, but we don't want Ebony to die."

"What?! No one better lay a hand on my daughter. That includes you, whoever you are."

"Well, tonight, I'm not the one you should worry about. It's your mother and your family. They are the ones who will sacrifice our daughter to the Dark Lord. But you can stop it. Only you."

"That's why you brought me back here? To save the daughter that you hate?"

"I have my own motives, but you must kill them all tonight. That is my command."

The lights in the entire four-floor basement flickered, and the sound of Malphas's demonic laughter shook the room. Evelyn cringed in pain as the sigil from hell ignited in a fiery flame on her chest.

"That is my servant's command, and you will obey!" Malphas's deep baritone voice sent tremors through her body, making her fall to her knees in submission.

"Fine. I tried my best to protect my daughter from this, but now I have no choice but to end it all for good."

Evelyn, now dressed in the white gown and black boots, draped herself in the long, flowing black velvet cloak. Her eyes burned a deep ruby red, flames of hellfire flickering in their depths as she stood confined within Malphas's power, waiting patiently for Cain's command.

Upstairs on the main floor, Wendell met with the old black server who had poured the blood tonic at the Diviner Women's table.

"Oh, here is the last portion of your pay. Thank you for your service."

"But what happens now? They drank all of the wine in both carafes but showed no sign…"

"Look, I just needed you to get it in their system. Don't worry about the rest. I have it all under control."

The man swallowed hard as Wendell leaned in closer.

"Keep your mouth shut, or I will kill your whole family—starting with you. Do you hear me?"

"Yes. I would never tell a soul!"

"Good."

After slamming the door shut, Wendell let out a slow exhale, his mind drifting back to his daughter. Holding her in his arms had ignited something in him—a feeling both foreign and familiar. As she lay against him, he couldn't stop thinking about how much she looked like her mother. Yet, her darker complexion and sharp facial structure mirrored his own. She reminded him of his late mother in her youth.

But now, he had a ceremony to crash, a ritual to end, and a powerful daughter to capture.

THE DEVIL'S BABY

CHAPTER TWENTY
The Devil's Baby

Ebony

I stayed in my room all day. I just couldn't bring myself to leave it. How did I come this far only to turn into the very woman I despised at times? I have been so upset with my mother for living a lie and raising me in one, but now I'm just like her. There's no way Cheryl could have brought me home last night. I know that, even though I was in a different mental state, she was killed by my so-called father. But when I walked out there and saw Miss Woods' terrified face, I lied without hesitation.

I disgust myself. The more I learn about my parents, the more I become them.

The dream connection I had with Mama last night was so intense. As I walk around my room, I realize that this is actually *her* room. I'm guessing Grandma Violet repainted it, and Mason and his staff redecorated the suite. Looking toward the large stone mantel fireplace, I remember my mother standing there, ashamed, explaining her actions to me.

I can't believe the murderer is my father. A wealthy man but extremely broken. A man who worships the devil, just like so many others in this town. Because for them, Sheiton was their savior, the only one who heard their cries when no one else did.

Centuries of torture, rape, incest, murder in broad daylight, and being forced to work for free under the worst conditions imaginable. They prayed to whoever would listen— whoever would *help* them.

I feel brainwashed.

The devil can't be that bad. He might be good—at least for my people. We still need protection, provision, and *some* kind of out-of-this-world power that will allow us to progress in this country without the fear of being killed—shot dead in the streets.

But if one believes that the God of heaven is real, then they *must* believe in the lord of darkness. Because you can't have one without the other.

That reminds me of what Mama said about Cain bringing her back to life. Through that resurrection, Mama and I were able to truly talk—to heal our broken, rotten mother-and-daughter relationship. If he was able to bring her back to life with the power of Malphas, Sheiton's son…

It makes me wonder…

What impact will *I* have on this family?

The Ceremony

The gust of wind blew cool air against her face. Eyes closed, she waited silently for her turn—to take them down and protect all that mattered to her.

Ebony.

"It's time."

She opened her eyes to see a monster of a man. Taller, stronger than the human version of himself. His breath reeked of fresh blood, and his muscular body was carved with stone-hard muscle. He walked toward Evelyn slowly, pulling out a key.

One key for every lock. As soon as she stepped forward, the burning sigil ignited.

"Where do you think you're going, witch? You don't move until *I* say move, you got that?"

Evelyn nodded, the pain radiating through her chest, the sigil branding her from the inside out.

One by one, he removed all the chains. But there would be no freedom. He grabbed her roughly, dragging her toward the truck.

Chained down once more, she sat in silence as they set off for the Temple of God's Anointed.

———

The Great Mother, Violet, and her granddaughter Ebony parked outside the church and, with lit candles in hand, walked along an old path deep within the heart of the forest. The air was thick with fog, and the shadows of gnarled trees stretched ominously beneath the full glow of the blood harvest moon. As they entered the clearing of the ancestral space, they were met with a flickering sea of black candles, their swaying light casting eerie shapes on the dark, mossy ground.

Standing in position, encircling the ceremonial space, were twelve cloaked figures—each draped in heavy black robes that concealed their faces, their hoods drawn low to create an impenetrable void where their features should be. They stood in eerie silence, holding thick, dripping candles whose flickering flames barely illuminated the cold glint of the ceremonial medallions hanging around their necks.

At the center of the circle lay an ancient stone altar, its surface carved with deep, intricate sigils of power and domination. Surrounding the altar, a massive ritual circle was etched into the ground, its lines filled with blood-red chalk that glowed faintly, pulsating with an unnatural light. Arcane symbols and inscriptions in a forgotten language marked the circle, invoking the dark power of Sheiton, the Dark Lord.

The atmosphere was thick with malevolence. The ritual was a cold-hearted reflection of the elders' ambition and insatiable greed for power. The Diviner Women, the most powerful coven of Black American witches, stood alongside their coven sisters—the powerful Woods Women—united in an ancestral alliance fueled by their shared lust for dominance. The mayor and other influential male leaders of Laketown and Old Laketown stood solemnly. When visible beneath their hoods, their faces were expressionless masks of determination, hardened by decades of wielding power.

Their motives were rooted in a selfish desperation to maintain their grip on earthly power. For decades, their influence had waned, and they saw Ebony's sacrifice as a way to reestablish their dominion. They believed that offering the blood of an innocent—one destined to become the most powerful witch of her lineage—would summon Sheiton's favor, renewing their strength and extending their lifespans.

The Holy Bishop, adorned in his ceremonial gold and black attire, stood as the focal point of the gathering. His eyes burned with a cold fire as he raised his hands, commanding the crowd's attention. His voice carried unshakable authority as he chanted incantations in a language older than time. His words sliced through the thick air, sending shivers down the spines of those who watched and listened.

Ebony, the unwitting lamb led to the slaughter, stood in the center of the circle, her vibrant crimson gown shimmering faintly in the flickering light. Her innocent beauty was a stark contrast to the dark ceremony surrounding her. She smiled softly, believing herself to be part of a sacred coming-of-age ritual where she would receive her ancestral magical powers—completely unaware that she had been condemned. Her dark, shoulder-length locs swayed gently as she turned her head, trying to decipher the chants and the distant gazes of those she trusted.

As the ritual progressed, the dark forces drew closer with every chant and every flickering candlelight. And in that moment, as Ebony began to sense the truth of their treachery, a dormant power stirred within her. The dominant force inside her awakened violently, causing a tremor to ripple through the sacred ground. The covens and leaders glanced nervously at one another, sensing an unsettling shift in the air. The Holy Bishop's chants faltered, and an unnatural silence fell over the forest.

Then, from the shadows of the trees, a low rumble grew, accompanied by the unmistakable scent of smoke.

Suddenly, flames burst forth from the treeline, licking at the air but consuming nothing in their path. Emerging from the inferno was Evelyn, her eyes ablaze with fury. Her form was both haunting and magnificent—her body encased in a flowing white gown that swirled with embers. Her reddish-brown curls were wild and unbound, glowing amidst the flames. She radiated a spectral energy, her rage palpable as she stepped onto the edge of the ritual circle. When she spoke, her voice rang out like thunder.

"You will not take my daughter," she snarled, looking directly into the eyes of her mother, Violet Bridges.

The Great Mother, normally calm and commanding, was momentarily stunned. She stepped forward from her position, her face pale with shock and disbelief.

"Evelyn…" Violet breathed, as though speaking her name would break the spell. But the moment of recognition was fleeting. Her expression hardened into one of resolve.

"You were weak. You abandoned your destiny, and now you dare return to defy me? You should have stayed dead." Violet's laugh was sharp and bitter, echoing through the clearing.

"Weak? I was betrayed. And now you betray my daughter. I will not let history repeat itself." Evelyn's voice cracked with emotion, but the flames surrounding her only grew stronger.

"You tried to kill me, Mama, and now you want to sacrifice Ebony for your greed. You call yourselves protectors of the bloodline, but you're nothing but a weak coven of liars and cowards."

Violet recovered from her initial shock and stepped forward. It had been over twenty years since she had reconnected with her inherited abilities, allowing her religious beliefs to suppress them, but adrenaline helped her power flare to life. The Diviner Women, sensing the conflict, gathered around her, their hands outstretched as they summoned protective wards and prepared for battle.

"We do what we must to preserve our power," Violet declared coldly. "You were too blind to see the bigger picture, and now you stand in the way of your own bloodline's survival."

The Woods Women stepped back into the protection of Mother Earth. In times of danger, they used their ability to camouflage, blending into the deep browns and greens of the long-leaf pines. Silently, they disappeared—never being women of battle or confrontation. But the Diviner Women weren't bothered. Their sisters of earthly power had done exactly what they expected them to do—run.

Evelyn screamed in rage, and with it, the flames surrounding her erupted into pillars of fire that shot toward her mother and the coven.

"Mama! Grandmother! Please don't do this!" Ebony screamed within the circle, but the fire and the magic force clashing drowned out her voice. Their battle had begun.

The forest erupted into chaos as fire and magic collided. The Diviner Women called upon their ancestral power, weaving spells of defense and attack, while Evelyn fought with raw, unbridled fury. The air crackled with energy, and the trees groaned under the strain of the forces tearing through the woods.

A deep, guttural laugh filled the air, echoing through the forest. The sigils on the ground burst into flames, and a swirling vortex of black and red smoke engulfed Ebony. Her scream echoed, but it was quickly silenced as her soul was ripped from her body, leaving her physical form crumpling lifelessly to the ground. Evelyn and the Diviner Women could do nothing but watch in horror as Ebony was dragged into the infernal realm.

"Ebony, no!" Evelyn screamed, but she never took her eyes away from Cain. Her command was clear—kill the Diviner Women and protect Ebony.

Amid the chaos, from the shadows of the forest, Cain stepped into the light. His monstrous frame loomed over the battlefield, clad in dark, battle-worn leather. His glowing eyes burned with ancient wrath. At his side was a massive sword, its obsidian blade jagged and sharp, pulsing with infernal energy—a gift from Malphas, prince of hell, rewarding his vengeance.

With a grim expression, Cain surveyed the scene. His gaze fell upon the Holy Bishop and the powerful men who had orchestrated Ebony's betrayal. Fear overtook them, and they attempted to flee into the woods.

Cain's voice, deep and resonant, stopped them in their tracks.

"Running will not save you."

Before the Holy Bishop could plead, Cain's blade cleaved through the air, and with a single strike, the bishop fell lifeless to the ground.

The other men screamed and scattered, but Cain moved with terrifying precision, cutting them down one by one. Each strike was fueled by rage—his mother's death, the betrayal of his daughter, and the years of pain he had endured. Blood soaked the sacred ground as Cain exacted his vengeance, his sword carving a path of destruction through the so-called leaders who had once believed themselves untouchable.

As the battle raged, Evelyn and Violet's clash reached its peak. With her sisters at her side, Violet conjured a massive burst of energy, aiming to destroy Evelyn once and for all. But Evelyn, empowered by Cain's blood ritual and Malphas's demonic force, absorbed the blow. Her flaming aura expanded violently, engulfing the battlefield in a consuming inferno. The Diviner Women, despite their strength, succumbed to Malphas's hellfire, their forms shattering under the weight of Evelyn's unleashed fury.

Evelyn's body, badly burned and weakened from the battle, struggled to remain upright. Her vision blurred, and she fought against the pain, using what little strength she had left to call out for her daughter. But Ebony was gone.

"Cain… Oh Cain, have you seen Ebony?" she asked desperately, her voice frail. "I can't find her… I tried walking, but I can't feel my legs."

Cain regarded her with a cold expression. "She has been taken to the Dark Lord now—"

"No… not the Dark Lord," Evelyn whispered, her breath ragged. "She didn't complete her ceremony…"

Blood pooled beneath her as her strength failed. Even in her final moments, her thoughts were of her daughter, longing for the child she had fought so hard to protect.

Cain knelt beside her, gripping his sword with grim finality. His voice was devoid of emotion.

"You have done well. My plan is complete."

Before she could utter another word, he slit her throat.

Ebony

I opened my eyes to find myself inside what looked like a nightmarish version of a Victorian throne room. The air was thick with sulfur, and the room was illuminated by a hellish red glow. Black marble floors gleamed beneath my feet, their surface etched with glowing veins of molten gold. The walls were adorned with macabre tapestries of torment and triumph, while towering, wrought-iron candelabras flickered with flames that burned an unnatural blue. At the center of the room stood a throne—dark, ornate, and adorned with jagged spikes—where Sheitan, the Dark Lord, sat watching me with eerie curiosity.

Beside him stood his most trusted allies: Malphas, the Prince of Hell, a demon general with a sharp and calculating demeanor; Maryan, the Princess of Hell, an ethereal figure who radiated both beauty and terror. But it was the presence of another, a mysterious new daughter of Hell, that dominated the room. She was an otherworldly being with midnight-black skin shimmering with veins of fiery red and gold, her eyes blazing like twin suns. She exuded a power that was both magnetic and terrifying.

"Welcome, Ebony Bridges," Sheitan said in a smooth, commanding voice. "In honor of your ancestral ceremony, I have set you apart from the rest. You are different, my new child, my daughter. You will reign and bring forth the future of my family on the earthly realm."

"But Dark Lord Sheitan, I don't know how to reign with earthly power," I replied hesitantly.

Sheitan looked at me with the darkest smile one could ever imagine. "So pure yet so intelligent. You see, I already know that, and I have a plan for your destiny, daughter."

The Dark Lord extended his hand toward the mysterious dark female and introduced her with an unsettling warmth. I wasn't afraid as they approached me.

"This is Onyxia," he said, his voice laced with amusement. "But you know her as Onyx."

"Onyx? Is that really you?" I asked in complete awe. She no longer looked like me at all. She was magnificent—a terrifyingly beautiful force.

"You will serve as Onyxia's vessel on Earth, acting as the physical body through which she will establish new alliances and reign over humanity," Sheitan continued.

"No, Dark Lord! I don't want to die!" I cried out, fear gripping my soul. "What have I done to deserve death?"

Maryan, Princess of Hell and creator of all mystical beings on Earth, including my ancestors, stepped forward. Her unnervingly serene smile sent a shiver down my spine.

"Daughter, this was your destiny all along," she said smoothly. "The culmination of your bloodline's power makes you destined for greatness. However, Sheitan's offer comes with a dark bargain. You must kill any remaining elders and their eldest children, ensuring the destruction of the old guard who betrayed you and paving the way for a new reign. You will return with your face but Onyxia's body, her gifts, and her nature. Each kill will strengthen your connection, solidifying the bond between you and ensuring her place as Hell's queen and true ruler on Earth."

Sitting in the presence of Sheitan and his court, I realized they weren't offering me a choice—they were informing me of my fate. I had no say in what was about to happen.

I had to admit, ever since my first encounter with Onyx, I had been both terrified and intrigued. My life wasn't great anyway. At this point, my mother and grandmother had probably killed each other. I had no family to go back to, no safe place left in the world. And I still wasn't strong enough to take out the man who created me. Onyx would make me a better version of myself in every way.

Honestly, I was tired of being afraid. It was time for others to fear me.

"Ebony and Onyxia, come forward and stand together as one," Sheitan commanded. "We celebrate your earthly rule. Oh, and by the way, I am adding a gift inside of you. This will take you to another level, enhancing your strength and heightening all four of your senses."

I surrendered to my connection with Onyx, the connection that had lain dormant within me since birth. She had always been a part of me. Now, the dark spirit within me, once silent, roared to life. The seductive pull of this demonic, otherworldly power wrapped around me like a vice.

And I let it.

A New…

I woke up curled in the middle of the sacred site, directly beneath the blood moon. Whispering female voices surrounded me, their hushed prayers weaving through the cool night air. But with my new vision—one that could pierce through illusions where others could not—I saw them clearly.

"Who are you?" I asked, my voice calm but commanding.

They continued their murmurs, their chants to their gods filling the space.

"I won't ask again."

One of the figures, a young woman with piercing amber eyes, stepped forward and lowered her hood. "We are the Woods Women, Queen. We are here to worship and serve you in return for our lives. We hold great wisdom from Mother Earth and her planet. We will be of great use to you and your future reign."

I studied her, my gaze unwavering. "What do you know of my future reign?"

"We were visited by Maryan. She told us of your power and your existence. We have come to be your coven, to aid you in any way we can," she replied, her voice steady despite the weight of her words.

A dark smile curled at the corners of my lips. "Your magic will not work on me, but you can start proving yourselves now. Bring me your elders—all of them."

A wave of screams erupted into the night. Mothers, daughters, sisters, nieces, and grandmothers were dragged forward, their faces streaked with tears, their hands trembling as they pleaded for mercy. The elders—the same leaders who had once held dominion over this land—were presented before me, their expressions shifting between defiance and despair.

I, Onyxia, daughter of Sheitan and Queen of Hell, am the future ruler of the earthly realm. Tonight, the elder leaders of this great land sought to betray me, but that treachery ends now.

Reaching into my royal cloak, I pulled out a gleaming, razor-sharp knife with a black obsidian handle. One by one, I slit their throats. The women screamed in horror, some collapsing where they stood, others fleeing into the darkness. Blood gushed in violent arcs, splattering across my face and hands.

And then, something new.

A taste.

A craving.

When the warm crimson droplets sprayed into my mouth, I didn't recoil. Instead, I let them linger on my tongue, savoring the richness like the finest vintage ever poured into a goblet. The taste was deep, velvety, intoxicating—like a dark cabernet aged to perfection.

I licked my lips slowly, my voice barely above a whisper.

"Umm… the future tastes good."

THE END

THE DEVIL 'S BABY

JOHNITA M. SMITH

ACKNOWLEDGEMENT

This story began within me about two years ago when I learned of my mother and father's betrayal. This story was created from pain and hurt. As a child, raised in the church, I was taught that children were a blessing and a gift from God to their parents, but in reality, that's not always the case. In my adult life, I learned that even though I was a gift to my mother, I was at birth and even now in my early forties, hated by the man whose seed I come from. It was a reality that my mother and her family tried to hide from me for my entire life —until two years ago. Their dark secrets were revealed, and I found out that the love that I thought I came from was all a lie. My father never loved me and hates me for just existing on this planet. But as adults, we have to learn to deal with the good and the bad of life and the family that we are connected to because that part is totally out of our control.

I would like to thank my mother for allowing me to feel every emotion, express every part of my truth, tell my stories in my own fantastical way and still love me, while I learn to forgive her and move forward. I would like to thank my supportive husband and four amazing children for listening and allowing me the time to write my novel in my sacred space.

I would like to take the time to acknowledge the best publishing team a writer could have, SHERO Publishing, led by my friend and mentor, Dr. Erica Perry Green. This group of amazingly qualified and brilliantly talented women has truly shown me the power of making my dreams come true. With SHERO on my team, led by their faith in God and their belief in my dedication and creative abilities, I will grow in success as a novelist and continue to make my dreams a reality.

To my readers, friends, family, and most of all to the amazing strangers enjoying this novel around the world, thank you for allowing this story to touch your hearts and minds. I have a desire to create amazing stories that feature Black Americans and highlight us in exciting ways. To me, our stories are magical because we are a magical people. Please know that this is just the beginning for me. I will continue to grow in my craft of creative writing, building my catalog one impactful novel at a time.

With Love from the Author.

Johnita M. Smith

THE DEVIL'S BABY

ABOUT THE AUTHOR

JOHNITA SMITH

THE DEVIL'S BABY

ABOUT THE AUTHOR

As an American novelist, Johnita Smith's passion lies in creating impactful and relatable stories that inspire readers to reimagine the world through the eyes of Black American characters, exploring fiction through the genres of fantasy, historical fiction, sci-fi, horror, romance and paranormal romance.

Johnita is a graduate of Full Sail University with a BFA in Creative Writing, a member of Full Sail's Creative Writing Club, and Full Sail Alumni Network.

She has a full plate balancing her life as a passionate author publishing two to three novels a year, being a wife to her supportive husband, and mother to their four beautiful children.

AUTHOR
Johnita Smith
JOHNITASMITH.COM